MW01281816

ALSO BY JAN SURASKY

Rage Against the Dying Light

Back to Jerusalem

The Sound of Unheard Melodies

THE LILAC BUSH

IS

BLOOMING

THE LILAC BUSH

IS

BLOOMING

A NOVEL

JAN SURASKY

Published by Sandalwood Press
Victor, New York

Cover design by Rob Wood
Wood Ronsaville Harlin, Inc.

Interior design by Susan Surasky
Larkspur Design

Library of Congress Cataloging-in-Publication Card Number:
TXu1-980-647

To truth, grace, and beauty –

May they ever flourish.

To truth, grace, and beauty –

May they ever flourish.

Heard melodies are sweet, but those unheard
are sweeter...

-*John Keats*

Acknowledgments

I would like to thank those who shared Civil War letters from their personal family archives with me.

I would like to thank City College of New York and George Mason University for preserving and sharing letters from Richard Frethorne and Elizabeth Sprigs describing their plight sold into involuntary servitude and brought to America as indentured servants in the seventeenth and eighteenth centuries.

I would like to thank Rob Wood for creating thoughtful, inspiring, and always beautiful cover art and Pam Ronsaville and Kassie Wood for their support.

I would like to thank Marcia Blitz for lending her expertise, quick wit and spot-on wisdom in creating flap and back cover copy.

Finally, I would like to thank those who patiently critiqued this manuscript and provided encouragement and support in bringing this tale to the written page.

THE LILAC BUSH

IS

BLOOMING

THE LILAC BUSH

IS

BLOOMING

Chapter One

Mama set up the table for breakfast. It was usually us kids who did that, but today was very special. The annual fair and circus was coming to Mayberry, a town of three thousand forty miles away, and we had to carefully pick what we would wear. It was our yearly chance to make an impression on the kids from bigger cities.

Not that the cities they hailed from were humungous, but they were way bigger than Mayberry. Mayberry was central to a lot of mid-sized cities, and anyway, the owner of the circus came from Mayberry. He never let the people from Mayberry forget how when he was a kid the other kids made fun of him because he was short and skinny and wore glasses. But, now he was tall and muscular, mostly due to his overcoming puberty and growing to a great height, but also because he had learned how to tumble and walk the high wire from the best performers he had found in Europe.

Caroline Ann, the oldest, known as Carrie, or Squirrel, mostly for her love of the hazelnuts we found along the nearby stream that ran behind our small orchards and fields that every spring held the seeds of our ever-changing cash crops, and depending on who was addressing her at the time, came bouncing down the old, creaky stairs of our hundred-year-old farmhouse in a swishy, navy taffeta gingham-checked skirt, a white peasant blouse, and a brilliant red satin bow which held back her thick, wavy, jet-black hair, which she considered her greatest asset, in a very perky pony-tail. She had just stopped short of winding it up and putting it in a French twist, a style Mama forbid because she thought it too sophisticated and too daring and too much like those trollops who wandered the streets at midnight in big cities who we had only heard about but never seen. We were certain that Mama had never seen them either, but she had long used them to scare us into submission when we wanted to stay out past eight or begged for a sleepover which all the kids from Mayberry indulged in.

Next came Georgie Boy, or John George, as Mama always called him. Being the youngest and the only boy in the family he was somehow more indulged, not really spoiled, because he had his chores to do like us girls, but he always felt he could be last to the table. He had carefully chosen his only pair of chinos, a cowboy belt of which he was very proud that he had gotten for his last birthday, a pair of cool sneakers which he had saved his meager allowance for, and a tee shirt which would rival the Marlboro man for macho.

Now that we were all assembled, Mama gazed out of the window.

"The lilac bush is blooming," she said.

We didn't answer, because this was a ritual Mama engaged in every spring when the robins returned to lay their eggs and the songbirds added their chirping to the early morning cock-a-doodle-do of our barn rooster. All reliable signs, but Mama gauged every spring by the lilac bush.

We children swiveled our heads, as if in unison, an annual habit we had formed to give Mama the impression that we found it as important as she did. We looked beyond the yellow checked chintz curtains framing the old paned window and out into the glorious sun-filled pasture next to the barn. True enough, the first blossoms were showing through the greenery of the bush. The most vibrant, deep purple we had ever seen. We had always agreed that their intensity was unrivaled.

Mama took a moment to admire its beauty, burst from a seedling she had nurtured that had somehow found its way to the back of the barn. And, its reliability. Then, she turned her attention to the old heavy iron stove that had been in the family for generations.

"Who wants buckwheat pancakes?"

The griddle on the stove sizzled and Mama stood over it, dropping spoonsful of batter with one hand while she stood with her trusty iron spatula in the other. Buckwheat season was short and Mama guarded her supply with fortitude. Ditto her supply of honey taken from the hives of honey bees which fed on the soft, pink blossoms of the buckwheat plants. Uncle John Turner, who helped run the farm, made sure that Mama had as much of a supply as she wanted of the beautiful, dark honey which showed its deep purple when the rays of sunlight coursed through its plain glass mason jar, wrested from Matt Archer down the road who kept bees.

Buckwheat honey was a treat. Not only was it Mama's bastion against all ills, being better for coughs than the pitifully thin, artificially colored cough syrup sold in the general store in town, it tasted special. It had an earthy smell and its malty, rich, molasses flavor was sweet but not too sweet.

Carrie was the first to speak. "I'll just have one," she said. "All the girls are dieting. It's a contest to see how many boys they can get to ask them out before May Day."

May Day, the last day of school before exams would determine who would have a fella for the summer months. And, pickings were scarce. Most of the boys had to help out on the farms and had precious little leisure time. And, they weren't always sure they wanted to spend it with girls. Going fishing with the guys and skinny-dipping in the many water holes around held out a lot more appeal.

"You're too skinny as it is," said Mama. "I don't know any boy worth anything who wants a girl who looks like a broomstick. Why your father was stuck on me from the time we were both sixteen. And, I had some meat on me. Where it counted. And, when it came to threshing time I could bale hay with the best of them. When it came to tackling or hitting a ball, or getting to the pasture first to catch a runaway horse, no boy could beat me."

Carrie fell silent. No one argued with Mama on this

topic. Especially when she mentioned Papa. Yes, Mama was sturdy and tough when she needed to be but when it came to Papa Mama had always been a marshmallow. When the threshing accident took him nearly five years ago now Mama pretty much fell apart. Mama's sister Maybelle had to come from Pennsylvania to keep us together. Mama's eyes still teared up at the mention of Papa.

Carrie looked down at her plate and accepted the two hearty pancakes Mama dished up and placed on the old yellow chipped crockery in front of her.

"How about you, John George? A growing boy needs a lotta help when it comes to a good breakfast. A good stack of buckwheats oughta put a few inches on you right away."

Georgie Boy looked pleased as Mama loaded his plate with a heaping stack of buckwheats. Everyone knew Mama favored Georgie Boy, but we didn't care. We all loved him anyway. He was fun and you could tease him mercilessly and he didn't tease back. And, he was always there tagging after you when you needed him most. On the days when you felt most down he was there to puff you up. And, when I lost my first fella to that stuck up Mazie who had just moved here from New York in fifth grade and who lived in one of those pretentious old mansions in town, I found a length of red ribbon Georgie had put on my bed when I was out with a beautiful wild daisy he had fashioned into a bouquet to mend my broken heart.

Georgie was our hope for the future. He was being groomed to run the farm and Uncle John Turner worked long and hard with him, putting him on the back of the tractor during plowing time, taking him out to show him how to plant the seed, and making sure he was right next to him up front when the harvesting machine came in.

Next, Mama unceremoniously plopped the remaining pancakes onto my plate. "Anabel May, you are last but not least." Mama always said this, and I tried not to think too hard as I noticed my permanent place. I would just for once like to be first, but we all had our places. A year younger than my beautiful, raven-haired sister Carrie, and a few years older than our youngest, I was of course the middle child. Not really noticeable at all. Less a beauty than Carrie, I was blessed with freckles and fine, limp, sandy hair and arms and legs that never seemed to stay in place. And,

I didn't seem to know any antics that would make me cute like Georgie.

I was the responsible one. Mama relied on me for everything. When Carrie was curling her hair or practicing eyelash makeup, even though she couldn't wear it out of the house, Mama would call on me to go over to the general store and get the sugar she had forgotten or the length of gingham old Mr. Barker had just called her about that he had just gotten in. But, Christmas was different. Mama never played favorites at Christmas. Every year we waited for the Sears catalogue and every year we spent months before we even cut the tree to pick out what we wanted. One year I asked for a doll that was every bit as beautiful as Carrie and I realized later on must have been way out of Mama's usual budget but she got it anyway and I had a great surprise to find her wrapped with a big pink bow with my name on it under the tree.

Georgie dug in. "First one done gets to ride in the back with Sailor."

"Now, John George, we don't need any stomach aches on the way to the fair," Mama cautioned.

Carrie stayed out of the fray as usual, too

preoccupied with how to nab a boy without looking like that was what you were doing.

"There's no contest here, Georgie," I said. "Everyone knows Sailor likes you best."

Sailor, the large black and white mutt that belonged to Uncle John and Aunt Mabel always went with us to the fair. Uncle John arrived every year to pick us up with Sailor in the back of the pickup.

"Okay, now everybody eat up. I want us to be ready when Uncle John gets here."

Mama scraped the griddle clean and left to go upstairs to change into the flowered sundress she always wore to the fair. That, and the big straw hat she favored to keep the sun from her eyes.

As for us kids, we could barely eat for the mounting excitement.

Chapter Two

The drive to Mayberry was forty miles over bumpy, back roads and potholes gouged out by the fury of the previous winter. But, the chatter of excitement drowned out the squeaks and squawks of Uncle John's pickup, an old model Ford which he had kept together by rolls of duct tape and the knowledge he had gained as an army mechanic overseas in the Second World War. Every now and then he could be heard muttering to the vehicle as it approached a rise or a bend in the road, "C'mon Elsie, you can make it!"

Carrie sat in the back guarding her nails which she had done up in a very perky pink. Mama sat in the middle between us girls and Georgie in the truck bed with Sailor, glorious in the sunlight and basking in the gentle spring breeze which ruffled his sandy brown hair and pointed Sailor's ears backwards.

Aunt Mabel in the passenger seat up front held court with Mama on the latest gossip while I pretended not to listen. The talk was all about who had entered what and who they thought would win. As for us, Carrie had entered her bread and butter pickles which she had been putting up since she was seven, Mama had entered her famous cherry pie, and I had entered a quilt with hearts and meadow roses and our lilac bush in the center which Mama had thought quite fetching. Georgie had entered his pig which he called Rosie and had hand fed since she was a piglet.

Uncle John had entered his feed corn as usual, which was a staple in our area, and Aunt Mabel had opted out, considering her position as the president of the local garden club and the consistent first prize winner at every annual state fair for whichever of her roses she entered reason enough to stay away from a mere county fair.

As we entered the fairgrounds, we were ushered very quickly by volunteers with heavy red vests and the name of the county fairgrounds written in big white letters across them to a spot along the very back row of the rutted field which passed as the parking lot for any event that was held in Onondaga County. The circus tents were way beyond the fairgrounds, almost out of view.

"Hey, Carrie, how 'bout coming with us?"

Carrie opened the window and waved. "Super, Lizzie! Be with you in a sec."

"Not so fast, Caroline Ann. I need to know where you are at all times so you will need to check in with us on the hour every hour. Do you have your allowance money so you can buy yourself something when you need it?"

"I do, Mama. But, every hour?" Carrie pouted her usual pout which meant the usual negotiations.

"Okay, every two hours, but on the dot. And, no sneaking away off the fairgrounds."

"Thanks, Mama." Carrie blew Mama a kiss as she raced to catch up with her friends who were already headed for the circus and the daredevil rides Clayton Ashton brought every year to impress his former tormentors and take their money.

Georgie had already jumped off the truck and was searching the fairgrounds with his eyes for Will, our trusty handyman and part-time field hand who helped Uncle John run the farm. Will lived three farms down from us and was often at Georgie's side, especially after Papa passed on, trying to provide that male influence that Georgie now lacked since Uncle John was often preoccupied with providing an escort for Aunt Mabel's many church and social activities. Sailor was already at the front of the truck, knowing if he didn't appear to get leashed up he was in for a scolding.

Will was Willem Hendrik Vanderwort, Dutch ancestry by way of London's poverty ridden East End and several years older than Georgie, which made him about three years older than me. His parents were dirt poor, but they had tried to make it in three countries and this was their last stop. Will had a cheery personality nevertheless, and he was a hard worker. To me he was a blond god, but to Georgie he was a pal who never tired of skinny dipping and fishing in the many ponds around us.

Though Will was built like the Marlboro man and had endless blond good looks, he was shy. Girls avoided him like the proverbial plague, shunning him for the jocks and the wealthy of the school. Will never minded, preferring to hang out with Georgie or Sailor, or his own many dogs, acquired through the years since he was an only child. I was his most reliable female companion, let in only if he and Georgie didn't shoo me away for some all-male fun.

"Hey, freckle-face, where's that kid brother of yours?"

Will had appeared round the other side of the truck,

out of sight of Georgie. I spied him first. I ignored his teasing.

"What's it worth to you if I tell you?"

"One ride on the carousel or the Ferris wheel. Your choice."

I pointed in the direction of Georgie and giggled, wondering how Will could have missed him.

As I fell in with Mama and Uncle John and Aunt Mabel I scoured the landscape for friends of my own. Nothing could be worse than being stuck with a bunch of grown-ups for the entire day while they gabbed and gossiped and ignored me. Luckily, after the first few minutes of discussion on who would win for what and why they shouldn't and who was related to the judges and of course would win I spotted Lucy Mansfield a townie who lived in the village in a small house on the edge of town with perennial peeling paint and no one to fix it up. Her father drove a truck and was never home. Her mother took care of a brood of eight and seemed never to be out of the kitchen.

Lucy was a middle child with mousy brown hair like mine always plaited in two long braids which hung down her back nearly to her waist and were neatly tied with two red ribbons put in by her older sister at the insistence of her mother who was determined that all eight of her children be well groomed and well-dressed despite their position at the bottom of the scale at the edge of near-poverty.

"Hey, Luce," I called as I delivered the loudest two-finger whistle that both of my fingers at the sides of my mouth could muster. Lucy turned around and waved, a little embarrassed by my decidedly masculine efforts to call attention to myself, but glad to see me nevertheless.

"Hey, Annie May, how 'bout joining us?"

"Swell," I returned. "I think I can win us a pixie doll at the rifle shoot or the basketball court."

"Great," she answered, as she took stock of the many brothers and sisters younger than she was who she was responsible for. "Ma wants us to stick together, but I think I can convince Marcy to take over if I promise her half of my babysitting money from the Thompsons who have me lined up practically for the entire summer."

As Lucy and I took off for the rifle shoot by way of the cotton candy stand I spied Carrie mooning around with a new boy I never saw before. She was still with her friends, but she was staring into his eyes intently and he was showing a lot of interest in her. I could only hope he was the right type of boy Mama would pass on, because if he wasn't, we were all in for a long, hot summer of fights and arguments, and many threats of grounding and suspending privileges. Mama could be fierce if she was scared for her kids.

True to my promise, I won pixie dolls for both Lucy and me. I was even able to outfox old Caleb who ran the rifle shoot every year and to my knowledge fixed the gizmo that ran the clay ducks around so no one could actually hit them. I got him talking about the widow Carson who was known for her apple pies and her ability to tamp a good amount of tobacco into a smoke. When he started shading his eyes to see if she was there, I ran behind the stand and set the machine to run on an even keel, setting it at medium to give me a clear shot. I figured he owed me.

As we left the rifle shoot booth, pixie dolls in hand, my mind racing to figure out where my prize would fit into my already cluttered room, the loud speaker began to announce the prizes for all the entries in every category for the entire county. Except for my quilt, which lost out to all the women of the town of Mayberry Quilting Bee, and Carrie's pickles, which lost out to a Mennonite woman who had entered for the first time, we Parkers cleaned up, Georgie's pig even coming in third against all the hog farmers in Onondaga County. Lucy's family never entered, since her mother was too busy to supervise, and the townies never won anyway, given their penchant for store-bought goods unlike the farm families who relied on themselves for most of their own supplies. I challenged her to a game of horseshoes to get her mind off of it and let her win.

"Annie May, what did you choose?" I swiveled my head to find Will grinning at me, his arms full of the prizes he and Georgie had won, most likely at the horseshoe pitch which he and Georgie were good at, and at the two-legged race which he and Georgie practiced every year during the down time in planting.

My mind raced. I truly loved the carousel but that looked too feminine for words. So, I chose the Ferris wheel. "I'll race you," I shot over my shoulder to Will. I said goodbye to Lucy, promising her lots of girl time over the summer, shopping at the market on Saturdays and learning how to paint our nails during a rainy weekend.

Will beat me to the circus grounds, his long legs

passing me handily, his perfectly chiseled body carrying him quickly to the entrance gate. We laughed at the silliness of it all. We bought our tickets and passed Clayton Ashton at the end of the table counting his money and laying the wads of bills in a fair-sized green metal box. Then, we headed for the Ferris wheel.

"After you," said Will with a sweeping gesture as he ushered me in before him onto the leather seat for two that sat under the canvas top of the modern Ferris wheel that Clayton had purchased just two seasons ago, an imitation of the first Ferris wheel ever invented for the 1893 Chicago Expo. I felt grand as Will pulled himself in after me.

As the attendant came around and secured the bar that held us in and Will handed him our tickets I decided to take stock of where we were. More carnival than circus the Ashton show was set up in the farthest field of the fairgrounds with the big tent set up at the edge, almost in the back field of the nearest farmer. There were few animals, but there were plenty of tumblers and high wire acts in glittery costumes and clowns who juggled and did funny tricks and came out of a small car with several other clowns all at the same time. There were women in beautiful costumes who danced and sang and arranged their costumes at the end to form an American flag. And, there was a seal who barked five times when asked for treats of fish and balanced balls on the end of his nose.

The slight gentle spring breeze ruffled my hair even as we stood still. My jeans and checkered shirt stayed put. Mama had hoped I would dress more femininely but she had Carrie for that so she let my outfit go. In deference to her request, I took a length of my hair and wrapped a red bow around it.

Will put his arm around me as the attendant locked us in and we took off. He had always been protective of Georgie and me but this felt different. I felt like a queen. I basked in the attention, raising my chin and letting the wind race through my hair as we took on speed.

"Hey, freckle face, are you scared?"

"Of course not!" I wrinkled up my nose for effect.

"Okay, then put your money where your mouth is. If you make it through without screaming, I'll give you my horseshoe set I won for beating old Asa Jensen three times in a row. He's been the champion for three straight years."

"Deal. It's as good as mine already."

We sat quiet for the next few minutes as we picked up speed and headed for the top and then down again. Will took in the vista and I could see him surveying the fields that were adjacent to the fairgrounds with what I thought was a great deal of pleasure and even humility. As for me, I felt like I was on top of the world.

Suddenly, without any warning at all, our wheel, which had us thinking it would be spinning us forever, came to an abrupt halt, its mechanism noiseless, its riders struck noiseless as well as panic replaced the rude shock. I sat there frozen as I realized our car was stuck at the top.

"Are you scared, Annie May?"

"Course not, Will. You know me. I can chase cows faster than any boy. And, I didn't scream."

"I know. Those horseshoes are as good as yours. Still, you look a little pale."

Will tightened his arm around me. I began to pray, not the church kind of prayer, but my own kind. "God, if we get out of this, I promise I won't be a burden to Mama and I will work real hard to stop giggling in church with Carrie when Reverend Morton gives those boring sermons." For good measure I crossed the fingers of both hands and put them behind my back.

Since we were still stuck I ventured a peek to the ground. Little figures, almost like those small wooden ones Uncle John had carved to put in the miniature barn he had once given us for Christmas were plowing and spreading manure as if we weren't stuck so far up in the sky we could likely see Heaven. People on the ground below us were buying cotton candy and entering the circus tent as if we didn't exist.

Just as I was wondering if I would ever see those swimming holes again I was so looking forward to cooling myself in for the summer the wheel started up with just a small lurch. The creaky hum of the motor began once again and we were rescued. Will loosened his hold on me and the attendant gave us extra spins to make up for it.

As our car reached the bottom and we were helped out, I realized that I would have to keep those promises I had made to God. Will was relieved as well as our feet touched ground. We went straight for the fairgrounds. The sun was lowering in the sky and we knew Mama would be looking for us.

As we drove back home, the sun readying for another beautiful sunset, we were all happy. Carrie had found a beau for the summer, Mama had remained the cherry pie champion, Georgie had won at the two-legged race and the horseshoe toss, and I had been let off at the ground of the Ferris wheel.

I was looking forward to a long, hot, busy summer.

Chapter Three

The summer of 1953 was a long, hot dusty summer as summers go, typical of the summers we face in the backwoods of the area known as the Finger Lakes, which is as far away from New York City as you could get for being in the same state of the USA. But, we never minded the heat, although we often sweltered in the 90 degree heat waves, because not only did we have a lot of swimming holes to cool us off, we got to look at the most beautiful scenery on earth, better than all the pictures I had ever seen in any of those glossy magazines Mama once got occasionally when she dreamed of exotic vacations with Papa. I had seen pictures of the Andes mountains and of beautiful green valleys in France and the wonderful seaside of northern Italy but none of them compared to the gorgeous hillsides and plains of the Finger Lakes with the beautiful trees and wildflowers that dotted them and the bluest of lakes that ran through them.

The summer was also a big one for Carrie. It was that year that she met her match in boys. Jameson Sloan Taylor was a New Yorker whose folks summered in Mayberry. They had been at the fair to open their summer home and prepare it for their annual pilgrimage into the depths of upstate New York, leaving a housekeeper behind to tidy up and spruce up the old white frame farm house that sat not far from the edge of town. Behind it was an overgrown field with daisies and primroses and all the tall grasses that blew in with the spring winds. Behind that sat an old greenhouse, repaired by the Taylors and filled in the summer with the rare orchids they tended to make them forget their high-powered jobs in New York.

Jamie, as he was called, had been smitten the moment he had seen Carrie. Her dark, good looks, her brown eyes as big as the proverbial saucers, and her tantalizing smile, made him forget all those sophisticated New Yorkers and the girls who had coming out parties with bands that had to be reserved for the occasion at least when they were in grade school.

Jamie was pretty much a regular at our house that summer, all with Mama's blessing. Georgie and I were dumbfounded, but neither Carrie or Mama seemed to notice. They were too busy thinking up things that Jamie would like, like a new recipe for an apple cobbler, or an old-fashioned chicken fricassee that smacked of country cooking the second it came out of the pot. In turn, Jamie charmed Mama with samples of his mother's orchids all done up with a bow to match the speckles or striations.

It was a hot summer evening when Carrie sat down at the foot of my bed. The stars were out and I could hear the crickets chirping through the screen on the open window. I knew there was something up because Carrie, being the oldest and enjoying that position, never sat on my bed even though it was exactly like hers and we had shared a room since I was born.

"Annie May, what do you think of Jamie?"

"Gosh, Carrie. I don't know. I never get to see him much. You two are pretty exclusive. You're always off somewhere."

"Aw, c'mon, Annie May, you know I share him with you and Georgie. He's here for supper practically every night Mama will let him and his parents will spare him."

"Well, he is pretty cute. And, he's polite."

"Gee whiz, Annie May. I mean more than that. Do you think I should write him when he leaves at the end of summer?"

"What does Mama think?"

"You know I don't ask her those things. You know she doesn't like to get into my personal business."

"I think he's a good catch. None of the girls have a boy from New York whose parents are rich."

"His folks aren't rich but they do have good jobs that make money and he's an only child so he gets a lot of things. But, that's not what it's about. I think I actually like him, Annie May. I never felt this way about a boy before. He's kind and gentle, and he cares about me."

Carrie's sincerity touched me. I didn't know what to tell her, but I knew it better be good.

"Gee, Squirrel," I said, using the nickname we rarely used since childhood, "I don't see anything wrong with writing him. Mama likes him, and most important, you like him."

"I'll think about it, Annie May. But, thanks for the advice."

Carrie almost leaned over and kissed me, so thankful for somebody hearing her out and most of all taking her seriously. But, she thought better of it and returned to her bed, fluffing the pillows and reaching for a fashion magazine to pore over before turning out the lights. We weren't really a demonstrative family.

But, for me, sleep was elusive after our little discussion. It was the first time anyone had to consider that Carrie might not be ours forever. Panic seized me. We wouldn't be that tight threesome we formed even more strongly after Papa died. Why Carrie even knocked Lulu Eisenbury down for insulting the pigtails I so carefully braided in the morning before school for three straight years and was so proud of.

I mulled all this over carefully because I wasn't so keen on growing up. It was too much responsibility. Mama had had a hard life since Papa died and she was often sad.

I turned out the light and tried to go to sleep but somehow it was more difficult than it had been before. The summer breeze drifted through the open window, the air now cooler and more refreshing than the heat of the hot and stifling early evening.
Carrie was sound asleep and breathing deeply. I decided to count sheep.

Chapter Four

I t was a warm summer's day when I crept up to the attic. Summer had gone well and Will and Georgie and I had spent many scorchers navigating the woods and the ponds to cool off. We also had helped nurse Will's latest acquisition to his ever-increasing number of dog friends, a husky-lab mix he got from the animal shelter in Syracuse that by all accounts had been the runt of the litter.

We named him Jester, a name we all agreed on, because he had a cute little patch around his eye that made him look like a medieval clown. It was a while before he could live up to his name because he had obviously been neglected and been confined to the animal shelter for some time but Will helped him to feel at home and it wasn't long before they bonded and Jester followed Will around almost everywhere. It took a while for Jester to trust us as well, but when he could, we all played ball and Frisbee and Jester chased sticks almost all the way down to the pond.

I had only gone up to the attic to look over some of my old things I had tucked away for safekeeping.

Somehow, I wanted to remember the old days, when Papa was here and when Carrie and I begged Mama for toothpicks to make dolls out of the hollyhocks we found growing along the back pasture.

I didn't want to admit it but I missed Carrie. I missed our giggling over the daisy petals we pulled to see who we would marry and the gossip we whispered together in the meadow on a lazy day when we were finished with chores. I missed the secrets we shared.

It was time to curl up with the old raggedy dolls Mama had made clothes for and the wooden wagon Papa had made me to cart my dolls around. Sitting among my old things that were so much a part of my childhood always gave me peace. It made me remember when Mama was really happy and when Mama and Papa would dance together in the living room under the Christmas tree and gather us children to join in.

I looked for the stick to prop open the only window. It was an eerie but pleasant feeling to be alone among everyone's cast-offs filled with so many quiet memories. I almost always found a treasure hidden away. As I searched I spotted a pile of albums all tied up in a neat bundle sitting under Mama's wedding dress. The note on top was addressed to Mama and Aunt Maybelle. Curiosity may have gotten the cat but I wasn't going to let that old tale stop me. I quickly pulled the note from its rose colored envelope and pulled open the note inside.

To my two darling daughters,

We have nothing to leave you but these old journals. In them is the history of our family which is your heritage. I know we couldn't provide you with all the things we wished for you but we tried to provide a happy home. Pa was always so proud of you girls. I know he didn't let you know it often enough but he used to brag about you down at the Ag store whenever he could find anyone to listen. And, he used to chew old Jeb Mayer's ear off about how fast you were growing and how Maybelle won the ice skating contest down at the old pond and how Marylee was turning out so pretty she would be the belle of the ball someday.

When you open this we will be gone but know that we will be with you in spirit. We wish for you a life that brings you as much happiness as you can find.

Your loving parents,
Rosie and Clem Thompkins

I stared at the beautiful script the note was written in which was Granny Rosie's pride. Everyone in the county vied to get her to address their envelopes come Valentine's Day or Christmas or very especially their wedding invitations.

Looking at the note brought back memories of lazy Sunday afternoons when, after church, we went over to the Thompkins homestead for a leisurely family dinner. There were platters and platters of food, the chickens and ham all roasted in Granny's big oven, the corn and the beans and the red potatoes all grown with Gramps' own hand. We kids played outside after the feast while Gramps and Papa outdid themselves in the parlor with longer and longer fish tales, settled in the old stuffed chairs and tamped down the special tobacco in favorite pipes that Papa had brought to please Gramps, often falling asleep before they could finish. Mama and Aunt Maybelle went into the kitchen with Granny to wash up and exchange the gossip which they had hardly been able to keep to themselves.

I opened the top journal and peeked in. It was labeled Great Uncle John in Granny's writing with a beautiful magenta marker on a strip of adhesive tape. I began to read.

January 1862—To My Dear Wife,

It has been hard to enlist and leave you my dear wife and my dear children and for my mother to part with her only son. It was hard to leave my job as a mechanic in Springwater and to leave our small farm. I was uneasy of the horrors of war but it seemed to me that those states that had rebelled under a government like this must be wicked and treasonable people. I have enlisted to save my country from ruin.

We march to Washington tomorrow from Elmira as the sun comes up. I have been chosen as cook by popular vote. Charlie Graham was chosen as my helper. He's a lazy sort, so I hope he perks up. Over a hundred men to feed.

Your Loving Husband
John Thompkins

January 1862—So my dear wife this is the last time I shall write you from Elmira. I am well at present and am hoping that you and the rest of the folks are the same. I want you to kiss the children and tell them I go south on Tuesday at 5 o' clock in the afternoon. We have got our guns they are the mini rifle they are nice guns. I sent you one dollar instead of two I left a half dollar for Mother with James and I lent a boy a half and we will pay it to you.

We shall go to Washington. I would like to see you well. You must be a faithful wife to the small ones as I shall be a good ways off through this. Tell Alfie I want that he should write me. My love to all and I want that you should write often as this is from your affectionate husband.

John Thompkins

January 16, 1862—Washington D.C. I will write a few lines to you. I am well and I hope these few lines will find you and Mother and my children well and all of the folks. I want you to send to Turner's shop and get my broad ax if you can and tell me how the coroners verdict turned out in the case of Caleb Brown. I would like to see you. I could tell some stories that I have fared well. The captain thinks a good deal of me and so do all the boys.

I got four United notes of ten dollars each they will help you some time. The news is I have two new cooks in the place of Graham he got lazy and some boys reported him and the captain wrote him a discharge. I am glad of the change. There was a death in Company G next to us. He was brought through the regiment in the hearse in the military style of arms. I saw the procession it was the first I ever saw in my life. He was a stranger to me. There was a small battle a few day ago the rebels lost 400 hogs and some men and arms. All troops is to make a grand rush this month the south must go down or the honor of the north is gone. I must close my letter as the hour of eleven has come and the lights have been ordered out a good while ago.

> Yours truly
> Affectionate husband to wife
> and mother and children
> John Thompkins

I will send you a gold dollar in this.

April 18, 1862—Today I am on camp guard. It is two hours on and six off. I have been thinking what was best for you to do. I want you to go and look to the worms on the apple trees and not let them hurt them. I hope that you have bought the old farm for we needed it to make us a happier situation then we can have all the pasture and a good place to raise all kinds of grain and corn.

I don't want you to suffer nor the rest of the family. I will have one hundred and fifty dollars due me and 16 dollars per month and the rest of my bounty. I like it here very well the water is good but the fare is hard. I have coffee and hard tack and some sugar. The meat rations are small. If only I had what we had thrown away but we can't carry it. The ground is covered with cotton blowing around here.

I would like to be there with you today but the time passes off. I want you to be as saving as you can this is full of love.

John Thompkins

August 13, 1862—Camden St. House—US General Hospital—Baltimore Maryland
My dear wife,
I set myself to write a few lines to you. I feel some better today. I have been quite sick since I wrote to you. I have had diarrhea. It has taken many men from us about twelve a week I have seen them die all around me. I am better now I can walk some. I can't get downstairs yet. I can't get a chance to see my family. I can't get the thought from my mind what I shall do. I hope that the Lord will bless all our efforts to help us in all our labors. My heart is with you and I can't forget you when the troubles pass over me. What will become of the one of my

choice and the sweet children. I intend to do all that I can for you and all the folks. I feel lonesome to stay here and not see anyone that I ever have seen. Will close with my love to all and kiss the little ones.

John Thompkins

November 1, 1862—Camden St.—U.S. General Hospital—Baltimore Maryland

My dear wife,

I hope that these few lines will find you well although I am in poorer circumstances. The Doc thinks I will fever again. I lay on my back and write this. I am in the same hospital I was in in August. Six or seven hundred of us wounded in the battle of Antietam. I have found some old friends here. I hope that this war will come to a close so that all the hurt can get home. I hope that you will not forget me. I could try to get discharged but I would lose my pay and bounty so I thought I better wait a spell. Write the news and tell me how you and your folks are getting along.

> This is from your ever thoughtful lover and husband John Thompkins to his wife and children.

November 18, 1862—U.S. General Hospital— Baltimore

My ever beloved wife,

Still will I write to you though I have not heard from you since the 17 of September. I hope that you have not forgotten me altogether. I feel some better now but the chance is small for me to get home but still I hope for the better. I am well treated here but still it is not home. I feel that I would like the comforts of my family and well would you like the one there would stand by you in hours of affliction. I for my part can say so for one word has oftimes cheered and revived my energies. It has pleased God to spare me for some humble purpose. I want to see my children and all folks near to me.

Kiss the children for me and tell them their father has not forgotten them. Learn them the things that are good for them and beneficial to their education. My love to you and all the rest of the folks from your ever loving and faithful husband to his dear wife and children.

John Thompkins

November 21, 1864 Chapen Farm, Virginia

My ever beloved wife,

I am well and my hand is almost well now too. I hope your father will come to Springwater and see you. If I can't come it will be some comfort to you to see your father and mother. I would like to be there to see them before they go west. This war is hard for me to bear and I hope it will come to a settlement soon as it can for I am tired of this southern soil. I can't help thinking how us boys has been used in the 28th battery. I hope that justice may be done us yet as it has been done to others. I got back and our quarters were all gone but the ground was left and stumps. Our regiment was moved to the rear of the old place some fifty rods. The Rebs make a dash to our left but it is short. I heard the firing it was five or six miles from here. It rains all the time now. I thought that the news of the president filled all the hearts of the north with a remorse of hatred to the offending murderer. It has been a sad blow. I am in sight of the Insane Institution that is a large stone building of immense size there is about 180 in it men and women. I have heard some of them talk there is a droll feeling in them they are mostly very smart as the war has made them so.

John Thompkins

November 1864

My dear wife,

I am so glad the fighting is done and Lee has surrendered to the union forces and that all we hope is the laying down of their arms and that lasting peace will be the issue of the Rebellion. I feel for my part that home suits me better than all wars and their triumphs. It will be a joyous time when all the lovers of homes and families arrive there.

I was weighed the other day in a grist mill. I weighed 165. I have got some Indian meal. It is hard to get in this town. There are patrols there from two brigades. I hope that the state convention will adopt all that the government wants. It seems that the situation of this place is in destitute conditions as they have nothing to eat and all their teams have been taken from them either by the Rebels or by our force. It is hard for them. We lay in a corn field. The fences are burned and all of the outhouses. All the boards we can get are used for our tents and our quarters.

Tell Alfie he must be a good boy and when I come home I will fetch him something nice. I wish I was there to help him with the woodpile.

All my love to you all and kiss the children for me.

Your ever loving husband
John Thompkins

April 29th, 1865 North Carolina
My Ever Beloved Wife,
I will drop a few lines to you hoping that this

will find you and mine well. I am well now. I have had a long march to get here. It made me feel rather old. I had the diarrhea some but well from it now. There has come an order to the regiment to put the state flag at half mast and fire a gun once in each half hour for thirty days for the loss of the chief magistrate and President of the Union. We heard of it three days after the occurrence. Booth must have been one of the greatest rascals in the wide world he and the gang of these desperados. It seems that the conspiracy has been in view for some time. I hope that they may be caught and be brought to justice. I think that this trouble would be settled by him in regard to the south better than anyone else but Mr. Johnson I think will come right to the point to them and all of the men found in arms against the Government will be treated as outlaws and rebels. Most of the citizens of this place feel thankful to come back to the old government they like the old flag and I trust will fight for the same. I hope that the tidings of peace will be published soon and all of the North and South may be united together in one circle of peace so that we all may be friends and bury the hatchet and that it will make us a happy and independent nation. May the blood that has been shed be wiped away.

It seems that as we are to guard the city of Raleigh we will lay here till we are sent north. We are drilled hard now for some purpose. It was a hard voyage. I hope we will be sent north but I can't say if we will be sent there or not. I have some boys here from Cohocton Elbert Anderson he says his wife will come see you some time but I can't say how soon. I hope that you can get plenty of wood and hay and meat and grain till I come back to you. If you go to the valley go and see James Ashton he can tell you about trade he will give you all the information you need concerning the business. If the fences will do then let them be until I come back. If you can help some in letting out the place to sow or pasture do as you think best.

My love to all.

John Thompkins
Your Husband and Friend in all trials and affairs

Please send me a newspaper.

The following was written in Granny's beautiful hand.

NOTE: Great Uncle John returned home in June 1865. He and his wife Abigail had four more children. In her diary the second child Caroline noted his passing as follows. "Papa died peacefully in his sleep on August 10, 1897. We had been with him the day before while he sat in a rocking chair and we talked."

In 1945 Papa and I traveled to Horseheads to attend a family reunion at Aunt Lydia's farm. We had a gay time. We set up the barn for square dance and Aunt Lydia's husband Uncle George was the caller. Aunt Lydia made her prize winning rhubarb pie and I brought the potato salad with the sweet pickles in it you girls always loved. Chester, Aunt Lydia's nephew, dug a pit by the pond and we toasted marshmallows under the evening stars and sang all the silly songs we ever remembered. There were almost four hundred people who traveled to be there that year. Over a hundred were direct descendants of Great Uncle John.

I closed the journal a lot more softly than I had opened it surprising myself with a gentleness I didn't know I had in me. It was eerie to look that closely into someone's life, especially someone who was no longer here. But, it was exciting as well. There were ghosts alright in this house, just as I had always suspected, but they were not the kind I had thought. The spirits of our ancestors were here in these journals and somehow I knew they were watching over us.

Mama had always said we come from strong stock. The answers to the mysteries of my ancestry lay in that pile of journals tied up so neatly with a thick red bow and laid so carefully on the old, rotting floor boards. My frolics with Will and Georgie would have to take a back seat to the summer reading I now laid out for myself. I tiptoed down the narrow, winding staircase that had been creaky since I was born, stepping carefully on the treads I knew were the quietest, and headed for the kitchen to see if Mama could use some help with supper.

Chapter Five

F all came all too soon. Mama liked her kids at home and not one of us was keen on hitting the books again, especially when nature was treating us to one of the most beautiful autumns ever. The leaves on the Maple trees and the Sycamores behind the barn and down by the creek were turning the most brilliant shades of red and orange, and the yellows and rusts seemed the most vibrant of any year. The soft breezes that ran through them and rustled their leaves ever so gently were still balmy, giving the promise of a fairly lengthy Indian summer.

The barn cats chased the small critters in the hayloft and toyed with Jester when he arrived with Will. But, Jester soon learned to stand his ground, and chased them under the porch when they got too frisky.

Once again, we were back at Baldwinsville Central. Though the janitorial staff had scrubbed the walls and the floors with ammonia, we could still smell the sweat drops from dazed and confused students attempting to answer questions like what year did the Revolutionary War end or where was Napoleon exiled in the sweltering heat of June exams. Or, so we thought.

The walls were still the same drab tan they had been since I had attended, painted with the thinnest coat of oil paint the staff could find. We still had cloak rooms with blackboards where countless students through the ages had attempted to answer math problems that seemed to have no answer.

It's not that I minded being back in school. I liked the girls, especially the ones from our village of Pottersville, which was in the township of Mayberry. Some of the Mayberry girls were stuck-up, and shunned us with their cliques, but others tried to invite us for sleepovers to see how the other half lived.

Carrie was particularly moody. Jamie had left for New York a few days before the school year began and their idyllic summer days had come abruptly to an end. Mama found lots of chores for her and insisted she finish her homework. But, Mama was not without heart. She took Carrie to Russell's apothecary in town to pick out a bottle of nail polish to save for special holidays and she added a letter box with the most beautiful stationary we had ever seen, all done up with

Carrie's favorite, red roses, with ribbons and lace along the border and even inside the envelope.

Georgie and I were beside ourselves trying to perk Carrie up. I offered to make her bed every day for the next four weeks and Georgie even offered her his very special stuffed giraffe on loan for at least two weeks but nothing worked. She continued to moon about.

As the leaves dropped from the trees in droves, and settled about the ground, scattering with every puff of wind, I lured Carrie out into the back pasture overlooking the meadow that every spring and summer produced the palest yellow of the wild primroses, flocks of white daisies, lavender violets and tall, lean spires of bluebells. Despite the brownish grasses moving in, the meadow still sported a number of golden yellow buttercups, a few purple bellflowers, and the vivid orange of the daylily.

"Hey, Carrie, time for some girl talk," I said, settling on the old log that had been knocked down by a big bolt of lightning some several centuries before, or so we figured.

"Gee, Annie May, I hardly feel like talking at all."

"Well, maybe not, but it's easy to see you're suffering from the oldest disease known to humans. You're acting like a lovesick cow."

"I didn't think it would be like this. I always had boys under control."

"You did. You were the best at it. But, now I think you've been hit by a stray Cupid's arrow."

"What should I do, Annie May? I miss Jamie so much. And, he's not even my type. I've always gone for the wilder ones. The fun ones."

"Yeah, Squirrel. But, you always went through them so fast. You got tired of them so quickly I thought we were going to have to move to find you a new batch."

Carrie tried to muster up a laugh but it didn't seem to go anywhere.

"Why don't you start by telling me why you think you have fallen so hard for Jamie?" I ventured slowly, moving only slightly toward Carrie to provide what I thought might be some comfort.

Carrie stopped to think and stared for a time into the far distance which was the haze of a beautiful horizon forming into the late afternoon as the sun got ready to set with its final show of reds and mauves, occasional soft blues and vibrant yellows, which I tried never to take for granted.

"I think Jamie is the first boy who has treated me with real respect.

"At first I thought he was kind of a reject. He didn't seem to fit in around here and he wasn't like those boys who visited here one summer from New York who treated us like a bunch of hicks. But, when we spent so much time together over the summer a sort of glow seemed to form. Jamie was patient with me and when I didn't know something he would explain and show me.

"And, he was so gentle. He never felt that kindness made him less of a man. And, when he first touched me, I felt a connection I had never felt before. Our first kiss was the tenderest I had ever known."

We both sat there in silence as Carrie finished her confession. Stunned, I contributed nothing. We had never been this intimate before. Without even feeling like it was me I moved closer and gave Carrie a hug.

"Annie May, I don't know what to do. With Jamie in New York around all those sophisticated girls I worry all the time that he will forget me. But, I know I have to look out for my future as well. Mama has made it clear that she wants me to go to college, at least to a secretarial school or something that can support me. And, I know it would be foolish to give that all up for something that isn't even certain.

"I'm no good at farming like you are, Annie May. I'm not smart like you are in school. And, I'm not funny and cute like Georgie."

I took a long look at the beautiful creature beside me and wondered how she couldn't see it too. But, I didn't have time to figure that out. All I could do was think about what I should say to a person whose thoughts had become so scrambled.

"Carrie, you are the most beautiful girl I have ever seen. And you know so much about fashion you can run circles around all of us there. You put up the best bread and butters in the county." I took a deep breath as I was about to continue.

"I know you are confused about Jamie. But, you have to have faith in Jamie, too. He seems very stuck on you, Squirrel. And, I think the year will show his character, too. Whatever he does it is better to know it now than find out later."

We both stood up from our log perch at the same time. The sun was setting and Mama would need help in the kitchen. It was baling time and the men in the family along with Will and a few hired hands were busy baling the hay and putting it out to cure in our largest and farthest field. There was nothing prettier than a field of round hay bales bound with twine amongst the gentle hills of central New York and the brilliant colors of autumn.

As we headed toward the house, its clapboards settling from almost a century of use, its shutters faded by the strong rays of the sun and its tarnished screen doors swinging on their hinges, we could hear the laughter and grunts wafting on the wind coming toward us from the barn. Haying was hard work and the men were determined to make it as light as possible. Mama always warned us that their jokes were not for our ears.

As we passed the barn, with Jester chasing the barn cats, his anxious barking a staccato to the unintelligible banter of the men, we knew we would be useful. Mama had promised Uncle John and the hired hands a hearty supper.

Chapter Six

Winter came with a huge snowfall in November. We had enjoyed a nice Indian summer until then, with the sunniest October skies, the mildest of days, and the lakes the bluest they'd ever been. Though the trees were now bare, the balmy weather made us forget the foreboding of an expected onslaught of the snow, icy roads, and just plain bitter cold that marked winter in central New York.

Georgie was happy because now he could use the new sled he had gotten last birthday, which came in May. Though Mama generally didn't get birthday presents of that nature, Georgie had had his eye on it in the Sears catalogue for months, so she decided not to wait until the next Christmas.

Farming was over but not the work of keeping the machinery and vehicles in good repair. Uncle John was over almost every day, his energies spent in cursing the trucks that wouldn't work and finding parts for the ancient tractor, spreader, baler, and whatever else he could find around the barn.

Will came over to help him when he could. But, for Will, school came first. Will was an A student and he looked forward to college and a chance to pull himself and his parents out of the poverty they had locked themselves into.

Georgie followed Will around everywhere, anxious to learn the secrets of making the old tractor start up without a fuss, or the old Ford truck purr like it did when it was new. But, he had homework too, and Will made sure that Georgie reported to him every day that he could when it was done.

And, Will was patient with Georgie. He wanted him to learn. If Georgie had a math problem he couldn't handle, or a science concept he couldn't understand because Mr. Miller was too lazy to improve his teaching methods, Will was right there to show him. It was many a day when I went to get something Mama needed out of the barn that I saw them engrossed with their noses in a book or Will drawing pictures or numbers on a pad while Jester lay at their feet, bored but happy. The barn cats had retired for the winter so he had nothing to chase but a few mice trying to make their way into the haystacks.

"Hey, freckle-face," Will called, as I entered the barn.

"Hey, Will." I answered, as I searched for the purple cabbages Mama swore were in the barn.

"How about helping me with this math?"

"You know I can't do that math yet."

"I know. But you can help me with the calculations and I can do the rest."

"Where's Georgie?"

"Up in his room doing his science homework. He'll be back for me to check it over."

"Okay, but it better not take too long. Mama's got me on kitchen duty because Carrie's got so much homework."

"Gee, thanks, Annie May. I have to ace this test. It's a big one."

"What are you going to do when you ace this test and leave us all to go to a big university?"

"I don't think I'll be going away. My folks need me here and I'm trying for a scholarship at Syracuse. That way I can commute."

I settled next to Will as he pulled out some paper and pencils to hand me for the calculations. He still looked like a blond god who was oblivious to his physique, muscles rippling from endless farm work, his good looks made ruddier by so many days in the hot sun, the wind, and sometimes the rain, driving the tractor in the spring, the reaper in the fall, coaxing the plants to grow with whatever fertilizer Matt down at Agway recommended, or spraying the latest herbicide to chase the insects away.

"What will you take at Syracuse?"

"I don't know yet. But, I will take a lot of science. I plan to be either pre-med or pre-vet. I love animals, but I know being the people doctor could pull my family out of the hole a lot quicker."

"Then, we won't see much of you, will we?"

"I don't think you can get rid of me so fast. I plan to help John out if I can. I'll need the money and he's always short-handed. But, Georgie's getting to be a big help. He's got a knack for farming that I've never seen in a kid his age.

"But, things are changing. I've got to realize I'll be the sole provider for my family. I've got to do a good job at that. My folks have sacrificed everything for me."

"I know they're crazy about you, Will. They brag about you all the time."

"I'll miss the days we've spent together, Annie May. You and Carrie and Georgie have been so kind to me. Taking me into your family like you have. I get so lonely sometimes being an only child."

"Well, you've got Jester. And, those other strays you bring home and mend."

"That's true. I don't know what I would have done without them. Dogs can be great friends."

As Jester heard his name, he perked up, scratching his ear as he woke, making both of us laugh as we realized he had just put an end to the most serious talk Will and I ever had with each other.

"Let's get on with the calculations."

I obliged, since whatever Will wanted I was bound to do since I worshipped him from the beginning. But, I also somehow thought that it was my job to keep him from getting a swelled head, so I proceeded. We finished as the sun began to set and I realized Mama was sure going to wonder about those cabbages.

Chapter Seven

It was November and the hills of central New York were covered with snow. The pastures and the fields were covered as well. The pristine whiteness formed a monochromatic backdrop to the very misty grey beyond.

The barn was locked and the chickens were in their coop. It was strange to see the hub of our usual activities so still and idle. But, it was in the winter that I found my greatest peace.

Mama was busy preparing for Thanksgiving when all the relatives were coming to our house. Although it was the most work she relished when everyone showed up at our farm, about every third year since Uncle John and Aunt Mabel hosted one and Aunt Maybelle and Uncle Elbert a third year. It made her feel just as important as before Papa died and besides, she liked to decorate with straw turkeys and the orange and brown coasters she had crocheted so many years ago.

Since it was a Saturday and all the chores were finished, I decided to take a stroll. Or maybe, a brisk walk. I decided on the latter.

As I set out for the back hills, a walking stick in hand, more for effect than necessity, I ambled about taking in the scenery. I was alone among the quiet, blanketed farmland. A very small cold figure humbled on very flat land that stretched for miles into what seemed to be nowhere.

I stopped and stretched. I breathed a deep sigh and exhaled. I could see my breath form a puff in the ice cold air.

I searched for the old barn of falling down timbers on the neighboring Taylor farm that housed their few animals and was only visible in the winter. It was a speck in the very far distance but I congratulated myself on finding it.

The snow crunched beneath my feet. It was a hard, crisp snow and very good for walking.

As I headed for the hills that rose behind our fields I saw a bright red figure pulling a sled with a dog trotting beside. Georgie. I only hoped that he had finished his homework or he would be in for a lot of caterwauling from Mama. But, Georgie knew his limits. Though he hated his homework, he tried to please Mama as much as he could, because out of all of us, Georgie had the most empathy. He knew Mama had it hard since Papa had died. And, Mama in turn had a glow of pride around Georgie that no one could mistake.

As I called to Georgie, Jester tried to answer. As I neared them, he stopped his incessant barking.

"Jester, what are you trying to say?"

"He doesn't want to ride on the sled, Annie May. Every time I put him on it, he jumps off."

"Well, he's just his own dog, Georgie. Jester likes to do what he wants. He's very independent. And, that's a good trait."

"Will said I could have him for the day. I thought we could go sledding together."

"It looks like he likes the snow. Maybe he'll give in and ride down the hill with you."

"Maybe if you're here, Annie May. I know Jester likes you."

"I know he likes you, too, Georgie, but I think he likes to run around in the snow and look for all the places he buried his bones.

"Okay. You get on the sled and I'll coax Jester onto

it and you hold him while you steer. I'll give it a little push to get it started."

As I watched the two of them whiz down the hill, their pleasure obvious as the runners of the sled blew up the snow around them, Georgie's laughter and Jester's occasional barking, I thought how lucky we were. A lot of kids in the village had to look for places to sled. For us, we had our pick of hills. And, I knew how hard Mama worked to keep the farm.

As they took their last ride down the hill, both of them tumbling off, Georgie doubling up with laughter and Jester running off to dig in the snow, Georgie pulled the sled up and plopped suddenly in the snow. I joined him.

"Annie May, why is everyone leaving me? All Carrie can think about is getting married, and Will is going off to college."

"They're not leaving you, Georgie. No one ever leaves anyone when they love them."

"Then why are they so busy they don't have time to play like they used to?"

"Well, they have lots of work to do to make sure their future is what they want it to be. I know it gets lonely sometimes. And, they probably aren't remembering what it was like for them when they were fourteen."

"Could you ask Carrie to help me with the lamp shade Mama got at a garage sale for my room? I want an airplane on it but I can't paint it. Carrie's a really good artist but she never has the time. I know she can draw an airplane because she made me a paper one once."

"Sure, Georgie, I can ask her. And, about Will, I know he hasn't forgotten you because he brought Jester over to play because he's busy with his college applications."

"I know Annie May. But, Will always built his funny snowman with me and we always used coal for his eyes and begged a carrot from Mama for his nose. We used to skate on the pond when it was cold enough and make angels in the snow."

"I can make an angel in the snow with you Georgie. Let's both jump up and down and see where we land."

As Georgie landed on the crunchy snow looking skyward, his arms making the wings of an angel, and I did the same, we both laughed. The clouds were beautiful as we lay there, the peace even more so. The vastness of the universe was ours just for a moment.

As we rose and headed back toward the house, Georgie dragging his sled behind him and calling for Jester, then hanging his sled in the barn, the aroma of hot cocoa and apple pancakes seemed to be drifting toward us along the icy air seeping out of every crack in the wooden supports that held together the panes of the old kitchen windows.

Chapter Eight

Thanksgiving brought a snowstorm and anxiety to Mama since the back roads were often full of snow. But, Aunt Maybelle and Uncle Elbert arrived with their brood on time even though they had to stay over in a roadside motel the night before because of a whiteout. Uncle John and Aunt Mabel arrived later with Sailor who always begged at the table.

Aunt Maybelle herded their four kids into the living room which she always called the parlor and set them up with games. She put the youngest in for a nap in an old crib we always stored in the basement for such occasions. Uncle Elbert made a beeline for the barn, even though the path was filled with snowdrifts.

Uncle Elbert was a steamfitter by trade but had hated giving up the farm that he had rightfully inherited but had no gift to run. He had agreed to move into town in Ohio's Putnam County with Aunt Maybelle on one condition. That he help out on the neighboring farms during planting and haying seasons.

When he and Aunt Maybelle arrived every third Thanksgiving and occasionally at Christmas he was certain that he and Uncle John could repair our entire farm in one day. There was always much bantering out in the barn and some good-natured arguing but there was never much work to show for it.

"Annie May, how about getting in here and giving us a hand?"

I swallowed hard and headed for the kitchen to see what all the fuss was about. Dishes were everywhere and Mama was trying to find platters and bowls to unmold the Jello and set out all the salads and sweet potato dishes Aunt Maybelle and Aunt Mabel had brought at the same time she was basting the turkey. Aunt Mabel was poking in all the cupboards, likely trying to find something to add to the gossip about us when she attended the quilting and garden clubs, and Aunt Maybelle was trying to find an opportunity to whisper to Mama without Aunt Mabel overhearing.

"Annie May, you can find a place for the pumpkin pie Aunt Maybelle brought and the apple rhubarb pie Aunt Mabel baked this morning. It's still warm."

"Yes, Mama," I said, trying to sound demure despite the confusion. "Is it alright if I set them up alongside the coffee pot in the dining room and then we can serve them after dinner?"

"Good idea, Annie May. Then we can pass all the bowls and the platters from the kitchen."

"How's your school work coming?"

"Good, Aunt Maybelle. I got honors in English."

"I always knew you were smart, Annie May. I'm so proud of you. You're a credit to this family."

"Thank you, Aunt Maybelle," I said, trying hard not to blush or wish I could fall through the floor. "Mama said you were good in English when you were in school."

"I was, Annie May. I loved English. The teacher always read my stories aloud to the class. I always thought I would do something with it, like be a reporter for the Newtown Gazette but I never went to college and then I met your Uncle Elbert and that was that."

"Well, you have a great family, Aunt Maybelle, and I bet they always like hearing you read a story to them."

"Oh, yes, they do. And, we make sure we read one every night. Why, Bessie's already reading a passel of her own and Luther will learn to read next year.

"Say, Annie May, can you find me a bowl for this cranberry sauce? It's going to melt if I hang onto it much longer."

As I rummaged through the cupboards for the right-sized bowl I thought how I would word the list that I would have to write for Miss Rogers, the math teacher who always suspended her daily math homework for Thanksgiving to assign us the task of writing what we were thankful for. I decided to put my list into a poem to please Miss Rogers because Miss Rogers was a gem. Although Miss Rogers never smiled, and was strict as the day was long, every kid who had her since the days she was fresh out of school passed the state finals.

As I thought about what I was thankful for I was interrupted by a fair amount of squealing from the living room and a few screams of "gimme" from Bessie and Luther.

"Annie May, would you see what that's about? Aunt Maybelle and I need to warm up the sweet potato casserole and find some marshmallows to add to it. I think those little ones are tired. It won't be long until dinner."

As I entered the living room, Carrie came in, a

queen in a beautiful green dress and fashionably polished red nails. All activity stopped as the former foes admired Carrie's outfit.

"Carrie, can I touch your dress?"

"Of course you can, Bessie. It won't be long before you're wearing one just like it."

"I'm not sure. Mama says she hopes I don't grow up too fast."

"Well, you will anyway. And, then you can choose the color of your outfit."

"I'm going to choose red. I love red. Do you think Mama will let me have red?"

"I think she'll let you have any color you want. And, with your dark hair, red will be beautiful on you.

"And, what about you Luther? What color suit do you want when you grow up?"

"I want purple. Purple is my favorite crayon."

Carrie laughed. "Well, maybe you will find a purple suit.

"Okay, who wants to play hide and seek?"

Bessie and Luther jumped up and down and shouted "I do" several times. Lucy, the two-year-old, just sat in the corner.

"Annie May and Lucy can hide together while you both look for a place where I can't find you."

As Bessie and Luther ran off giggling, I knew one thing I was thankful for. That Carrie hadn't run off to get married but had decided to stay and think about college. We would have her for one more year.

As Carrie and I looked for Bessie and Luther, who were very good at hiding, Uncle John and Uncle Elbert straggled in, much the worse for the several shots of whiskey they had already enjoyed while discussing how to repair the farm. Georgie followed, quite puffed up by the all-masculine company he was allowed to join.

As we rounded up the kids, taking baby Emma from her crib, Mama walked into the dining room, proudly carrying the beautifully browned turkey set perfectly on the platter decorated with turkeys and pumpkins, acorns and fall foliage, which she displayed the rest of the year in her prized corner curio cabinet.

Mama gave Georgie all of the honors for carving, setting the turkey at the head of the table where Uncle John could keep an eye on him. Georgie was pleased as all eyes were on him, using his whittling skills that Will had taught him to carefully separate the wings and the thighs and the legs everyone would inevitably fight over. Sailor watched him, tail wagging, trying not to drool at the aroma which wafted through the dining room.

"Who wants the wing?" Mama asked, as the little ones all yelled their choices. Mama tried to be fair, even remembering who had what last year. I marveled at how she could use such wisdom while remembering what went into the best sweet potato casserole she made every year from scratch. Carrie got the wishbone and shared it with Georgie. As they pulled and fought about who got the larger half, I found myself wishing as well. I wished that both their wishes would come true.

As Uncle Elbert tried not to snore and Uncle John's head kept nodding, I looked at Sailor asleep in the corner, full of the scraps everyone kept sneaking to him when they thought no one else was looking. As everyone ate, I made up my Thanksgiving poem in my head. I knew I would need the extra time to give those little ones sleigh rides after the dishes were washed and dried so they could tire themselves out before the long ride home.

Chapter Nine

A s I looked at the heavy snowflakes through the frosted window of the bedroom I shared with Carrie, I knew that it was time to visit the pile of journals so lovingly placed in the attic but so forgotten over time. It was now my private stash and each new surprise that awaited me brought goose bumps as my curiosity mounted.

It was Christmas vacation but there were many school projects that needed tending to. Georgie had a shop project and he named me sole provider of the proper tools to make it with. He had picked a small round-seated stool with three legs to create, and I was down at the hardware shop in town every Saturday since he began talking to Norm Stafford who had promised early on to help us. I became an expert in sanding and staining, as well as turning wooden legs for just about any piece of furniture you could name.

My own project was simpler. We had to write a book report on Dickens' "A Christmas Carol" but then we had to write a Christmas story of our own. As Scrooge and Tiny Tim took their place in my head, at least for a while, I contemplated the impact of the ghost of Christmas past and the plight of Tiny Tim and Scrooge's eventual transformation.

In this book there was absolute proof that ghosts could have an impact. I was certain they could, because I knew Mama thought about her own Mama and Papa every day and often told us stories her own parents had told her about ancestors she had never known. She often regaled us with these stories when she had a moment or when we were doing our kitchen chores together.

I left the old door that Georgie had cut in half and carefully shellacked, setting it on four big logs from the maple tree that had sadly gone down in a frightening thunder storm, complete with the rapid lightening that narrowly missed our kitchen, that I now called my desk, and headed for the attic. Carrie was at Lizzie's in town, most likely chattering non-stop about boys, and Georgie was busy completing his homework so that Will, who still looked after Georgie despite his busy schedule, could check it over when he got a free moment. Mama was busy at the kitchen table, checking her Christmas card list and the gift list she always kept in a secret place.

The attic, though unheated, was cozy. The pile of journals still lay in the corner, untouched since I had opened the first one. I pulled the second one out, gingerly untying the heavy red twine that held its old pages together. I settled against the beams that held the roof up, pulling an old Navaho blanket around me that had only a few large holes and found a pillow to sit on. I began to read.

Dear Rosie,

Though you are only seven, I am penning the tale of one of your ancestors, your great-great grandmother on your father's side, whose name was Aiyanna, so you will always know where you came from.

Aiyanna, who was born to a Seneca Indian woman named Adoette, a name that means "strong as a tree" in the Seneca language, and a white trader, was a half-breed. Her mother was a full-blooded Indian who lived with her Seneca tribe but lived with the white trader named William in a small cabin near her village when he was not away on business. The Seneca overlooked the intrusion of William into their carefully guarded social traditions because William was a skillful trader and brought into their tribe many wondrous goods for very little wampum.

Aiyanna, whose name means "forever flowering," grew strong and beautiful despite the hardships of her gypsy life. When she was with the Seneca, she worked hard with the other children in a communal way. When she was with her mother and William, though she worked hard alongside her mother to fetch water from the well for the few dishes William had provided for them, and to launder the few clothes her mother, who was deft with a needle, had so lovingly crafted, they were free to sit around the cabin at night, the kerosene lamp providing them a dim but eerie light. On those nights, William would play the harmonica, and Aiyanna would dance, often a wild dance as William's tunes became louder and faster.

Aiyanna grew like a weed, a beautiful flowering weed, often taller than the other children her own age, and often more spindly. But, when she began to mature, and became part of the Seneca maiden's rites, it was plain to see that she would grow to be a very beautiful woman.

Aiyanna would have been married to an Indian chief, either a Seneca, or one of another tribe, if Adoette had not borne her by the white trader William. Adoette was the daughter of a very powerful Iroquois chief who was forever being scolded by the elders for not having been strict enough with his only daughter and allowing her to think she could break the very strict Seneca traditions of marriage.

Adoette's father, whose name was Cheveyo, which means spirit warrior, had many sons, very much prized by Indian tradition, but he had always had a soft spot for his only daughter. So, it just seemed natural that he would have one for Aiyanna as well. On the rare visits when she was allowed to visit him in his tent, when he was not in council or leading a party to the hunting grounds, or at war with an enemy tribe, she would sit with him cross-legged as he sat, and they would talk about the healing herbs all about them, or the fields of maize that the Indians grew to reap and pound into a very delicious bread. He would especially tell her the tales of the Indian myths so she would know them, and not forget her heritage. Cheveyo was very proud of Seneca tradition.

At each visit, he would slip some trinket into her hands for her to keep in the small leather box William had given her when she was ten, for she was not yet allowed to adorn herself as a full-grown woman. Often, when she was away from the Seneca at William's cabin, and she was tucked into the small bed William had crafted for her, and the moonlight was streaming through the unshuttered windows, she would reach for the leather box and count the trinkets, all covered with the beautiful, colored beads of ancient tradition strung by the skilled hands of Seneca women.

As Aiyanna grew, she became increasingly restless. Although she adored Cheveyo and was inspired by the ancient teachings of the Indians, she had also great admiration for the rough and tumble ways of William, who survived in a land foreign to him for he had been captured at the age of eleven in his native Ireland and brought to America as an indentured servant. He had escaped his servitude at fifteen and from then supported himself as a very canny trader and a trapper when necessary. William's skill at trading was sought as far west as there were white men to trade with the Indians.

William was respected by the white men who sought his trading skills as well as the many different Indian tribes who sought the guns, the tobacco, and the beautiful fabrics of the white settlers. As a result of his travels   William   was knowledgeable in several different Indian dialects and several native languages of the settlers which he taught Aiyanna as she grew.

Despite his harsh background, William was very gentle with Aiyanna. He patiently taught her to swim in the old swimming hole out back and he taught her to wield both a gun and a bow and arrow, because Indian women were forbidden the weapons of battle. He patiently whittled her playthings in her early years and more utilitarian objects and adornments as she reached adolescence. She especially prized a doll she had named William even though it was an obvious likeness of her.

When Aiyanna was seventeen she ran away, unsure of her heritage, and built a cabin far into the woods. Both Cheveyo and William were heartbroken and William vowed to find her but Adoette, understanding her daughter's torment, convinced him to let her be. There she found a trapper named Abraham who cared for her as best he could. She bore a daughter she named Leotie which means "prairie flower" but lost Abraham to a tree-felling accident. In her grief, and unable to care for her daughter, she gave the baby to a barren woman in town who promised to care for her as her own.

But, Aiyanna missed the child, grieving for her every night as the sun went down and climbing the hills around her cabin as the moon came up, dancing the wild dances of her childhood and calling Leotie's name. When Adoette fell ill, William came to fetch Aiyanna, but when they returned to William's cabin, Adoette had died. Aiyanna grieved for the woman who had given her life and had taught her compassion but returned to her cabin to be closer to her daughter.

As the years passed, many men came and went in Aiyanna's cabin, unable to understand or to cope with Aiyanna's wild ways. When Leotie, now called Lottie, grew to be eighteen she learned of her heritage and visited Aiyanna, now ill and old before her time, but still beautiful. Lottie cared for Aiyanna, bringing her broths she had made and heated them over an open fire, and often a freshly baked bread.

As Aiyanna lay dying, her tuberculin cough taken hold of her and her body racked with the labors of survival, Lottie stroked her long gray hair, once silky and black as the evening sky, and soothed her weathered face. When she died, Lottie carried her to her adopted family's graveyard and buried her there.

Lottie married the only merchant in town and bore eight children. Her husband's business prospered, buoyed by the fact that, although her hair was a deep and beautiful auburn like her grandfather William, her striking beauty was a carbon copy of the woman known as a half-breed who had given her birth. Settlers traveled from all over to purchase the beautiful fabrics that

Lottie's husband went east to hand-pick, and that Lottie wore so well. Beautiful silks from Spain, woolens from the looms of the Irish, and brightly colored linens and cottons spun from the flax and the plants of the American colonies and dyed the brilliant hues of the roots, the berries, and the wildflowers scattered about.

And every year, on the anniversary of her birth, Lottie placed a wild rose on the simple grave of Aiyanna.

Lottie was your Papa's great-grandmother.

I gingerly tied the heavy red twine about the old, yellowed pages as they had originally been bound, careful not to disturb the tortured spirit of Aiyanna, the beautiful half-Indian maiden. I was both pleased and stunned that our lineage went back to the Iroquois. The once powerful nation, though depleted in number and its descendants now relegated to a Buffalo reservation, had left its mark. Though they had been run off their lands, and no longer hunted the buffalo, the beautiful and plentiful lakes that had provided them the speckled trout and pink salmon to cook over an open fire and on which they often paddled their dugout, bark canoes, still retained the names they had given them. We had swum in Cayuga, Oneida, and Keuka Lakes. We had once taken a ride on a paddleboat on Lake Ontario. Echoes of the Indian past rode with us, and the same cold, deep waters we swam in had taken the Iroquois to lands far west.

I felt so much a part of history as I placed the journal's pages back into place among the pile.

I walked silently down the attic stairs, the creaks barely noticeable as I placed yet another ancestor into the fabric of our very patchwork family legacy. I decided to check on Georgie. He was fast asleep over his pile of books and half-done homework. I roused him gently and put him into his bed. As I hugged him goodnight, and threw imaginary sand in his eyes to insure the arrival of the sandman who I assured him would put him to sleep immediately, I looked out through the panes of the casement window at the very full moon, the same one that had lit the journeys of our ancestors for millennia before us.

Chapter Ten

There were precious few snowflakes on Christmas morn but the frosted window panes we had so lovingly dabbed with thickened soap flakes and a sponge had made up for the eerie lack of Christmas cheer. We had declined an invitation to spend Christmas with Aunt Maybelle and her brood because Carrie was expecting Jamie for a visit the day after Christmas and nothing short of a presidential mandate would convince her to leave the preparations she was making.

We were all aware that this was the last Christmas we would spend together before Carrie went off to college and there was an unspoken sadness among us. But, we didn't want to break Carrie's excitement in choosing a course of study, or her dreams for the future of which she had so many. She would be a great fashion designer someday. Or perhaps the wife of a famous doctor. Or head a great charity and be revered by all the needy.

I went into our shared bedroom to find Carrie

painting her nails and looking about as blue as she could be.

"Hey, Squirrel," I said, as compassionately as I could so as not to startle her, "why the long face?"

"I don't know, Annie May. I'm happy that Jamie is coming to spend the rest of the holiday with us. I have been looking forward to it since the fall semester.

"But, I'm worried as well. I don't know what he's coming to tell me. He starts Harvard in the fall, and I know a girl like me from the boonies won't stack up to the sophisticated girls he'll meet in Boston.

"And, I have my own conflicts as well. I know I'll meet a lot of boys myself and I'm so undecided in a career. I just don't know what to think."

"Well, worrying about it won't help. But, if there's anything I can do to help you get ready for Jamie, I will. I'll even go shopping with you in town and help you pick out anything you want me to. I saw a really great crimson scarf with tiny roses and anemones on it on sale in Mr. Harter's window that would set off your snow jacket and make any boy take notice. Maybe if you take him sledding up on Strawberry Hill and ice skating on the pond out back he'll melt enough to tell you what he's thinking.

"You know, Squirrel, sometimes the future takes care of itself. With a little bit of wisdom, and a certain amount of faith, sometimes it will show its hand in ways you couldn't have imagined. And, if you're open to it, it might be worth waiting for."

Carrie just stared straight ahead, but her glum demeanor lifted and the bright Carrie I once knew, full of sunshine and the love of life, reappeared. She got up and gave me a hug and it was then I knew that Carrie had been divided too. Her whole life ahead of her, and the excitement that went along with it, had been marred by the same sadness that had plagued the rest of us. It was she who would be the first to be torn from the cradle of security. She had been afraid to crack that plucky and rebellious façade of hers for fear of seeming weak or a coward.

"Gee, Squirrel, we'll be right behind you. You know Georgie won't let you go because he needs you. You're the only one who can do all his art projects with him. And, who can I trust with my deepest secrets but you?"

Carrie sat down again to dry her nails and apply a third coat of polish. The sun burst through the windows and into the room with a vengeance, drying

Carrie's nail polish but ruining Georgie's plans for a Christmas snowman. Nevertheless, I decided to scoop up all the remaining snow that had fallen in a pile behind the barn in the shade of the overhang and bring it to him on the sled to fashion a small Santa Claus.

As we sat, our private thoughts of the future plaguing us silently, Georgie burst into the room, his face a picture of panic and consternation.

"Carrie, can you draw me a picture of a car? We need to tell how to fix the brakes and where they are for shop. I know how because Uncle John showed me. But, I can't draw it. And, we have to have it done by the first day of school after vacation."

"Of course I will, Georgie, but first I have to let my nails dry. Why don't you take a look at the new art book I bought. You might find some cars in there."

As Georgie occupied himself with Carrie's new art book and a look of relief replaced the look of panic, I tiptoed out to make my way down to the kitchen where I knew Mama was bustling around to prepare what she knew were Jamie's favorite foods. I didn't know how she had done it, but Carrie had somehow managed to have Jamie work his way into Mama's favor without her knowing it. And, Mama was hardly a soft touch.

When I arrived in the kitchen, Mama had several bowls and a casserole for Jamie's favorite stew. "How about I mix up the lime Jell-O for the pineapple and cottage cheese mold, Mama," I offered.

"Very good, Annie May, and we can put you to work doing the slaw as well. I think I'll put a batch of fried chicken in the deep freeze out back in case anyone gets hungry later.

"And, if you get to it, you can mix up some chocolate for a thermos of hot cocoa and dig up the marshmallows to go with it.

"We'll need to set up a cot in the parlor, as your Aunt Maybelle calls it. Jamie needs his privacy."

As I worked alongside Mama it only made me lonelier with the thought that Carrie would be going off to college in September. Mama never addressed anything unless you brought it up to her. And, I was determined not to bother her or look like a coward who couldn't handle even her own problems. But, I sensed Mama could tell.

"You know, Annie May, I think we should make this a special holiday since it will be Carrie's last

Christmas before she starts college. But, I think she's pretty set on Wells so she won't be far. She can get a job on campus there and she can be home as often as she can. I know she'll miss your steady hand when things pile up and I'm sure Georgie will be begging for her help in all his art projects."

I felt better that Carrie would be that close. If she got homesick, I knew Uncle John would go fetch her for a home cooked meal. Uncle John had always spoiled Carrie and he was the only one who would put up silently with her sometimes flighty ways. As the oldest, Carrie had been close to Papa, and although he had never played favorites, I knew he had set his sights on Carrie.

Carrie did buy the crimson scarf in Mr. Harter's window and it gave just the right touch to her deep blue snow jacket with the lavender trim. Carrie looked like a snow queen when she set out with Jamie for sledding on Strawberry Hill.

As we gathered around the table for supper the night Jamie arrived and waited to open presents after supper, I never did find out what words Carrie and Jamie had shared on Strawberry Hill or out back on the pond where they skated for a very long time. I only knew that as we sat, exchanging stories from the year since Jamie had left at the end of summer, Carrie sat next to Jamie and she looked very, very happy.

Chapter Eleven

W ill was just as handsome as ever, and just as
unassuming, as he helped Uncle John tow the
tractor out of the barn for some much needed repair
work. It was spring, and planting would soon begin.

Will's muscles fairly rippled beneath his tee shirt as
he sat in the truck with the tow on it and helped to
haul the tractor out into the sunlight on a very
beautiful spring day. I could hear the birds chirping
non-stop as they issued directions to their mates and
carried straw and twigs and whatever they could find
to build a suitable nest to raise their young in. Nests
were everywhere, under the roof of the barn, out back
high up in the cherry tree and in the crabapple, both
with their white blossoms ready to burst, and in many
of the trees that grew out back on Strawberry Hill. It
had been a regular spring activity in our younger years
to drag a ladder to the back acres and search for birds'
nests to see the different colored eggs, with their pale
blues and browns, some as pure as the blue of the
robin's egg, some as blotchy and spotted as the
cardinal's, the scrappy blue jay's, or the chickadee's

and the nuthatch's. If we were quiet in the kitchen we could often look out the window and watch them carry food to their fledglings who were chirping so loudly with hunger.

As I stood off to the side watching Uncle John and Will, and Georgie who was always ready to assist, struggling with the tractor to get it to behave, and pulling every tool they had out of the tool shed in hopes that one would work, I felt a certain pride. Although I wasn't included in spring planting, I felt an excitement just as if I was. For spring planting was like welcoming a new baby into the fold, a newness that was filled with hope.

Our fields would soon be filled with the seedlings of beans and corn, hay and a small patch of pumpkins. Uncle John had even decided to grow onions and potatoes this year. And, we kids would have our own garden of tomatoes, three different kinds of lettuce, cukes and peppers. But, no matter how hard Uncle John and his hired hands worked, I knew we owed our harvest to the vagaries of the weather. I silently prayed for rain.

"Hey, Annie May, don't just take up space. Go get my lug wrench out of the barn." Uncle John was anything but gentle when he was preparing spring planting.

"Where is it, Uncle John?"

"After all these years you should know it's hanging up over the work bench."

I searched and searched the wall along the work bench but saw no wrench of any kind. I returned to look at the mess of tools at Uncle John's feet and retrieved the lug wrench.

"Thanks, Annie May. If you work it right, you could be pretty good at farming yourself. My Aunt Bertha worked the land after my Uncle Calvin passed away and got a pretty good yield at that. She was the only woman in these parts to get out on a tractor and haul a spreader, but she could regale you with stories about how she outwitted the crows and the rabbits and just about every pesky critter that crossed her path."

"Thanks, Uncle John, but I'll stick to my plans for college. I want to be a teacher."

"Well, you'll have to be good with the books and study hard. But, I know you can do it. You've got a will of iron, Annie May."

"I want to teach in college."

"Well, you always did have big ideas. But, nothing

wrong with big ideas. Your Papa was a dreamer too. He had in his mind to buy the Taylor farm next door, hire more hands and be part of a big supply chain to keep all the upstate supermarkets in produce."

At the mention of Papa my heart went mushy because every day I wished he was here. But, instead, I asked Will if when he was finished he would walk back with me to Strawberry Hill and help me pick some berries for pie tonight. Though he was oozing sweat and his muscles were straining to tighten the bolts to fasten the new hydraulic cylinders Uncle John had just purchased down at the new Agway just put up on Route 34 and to get the old crankshaft purring, he looked up and nodded with his usual, agreeable smile.

I went in to the barn to fetch the tin pail we used to use to milk Maizie before Mama decided it was cheaper to buy milk from Alton's down the road and Maizie went to a large dairy farm upstate. We missed her, because she was every bit our companion as well as our milker. She would begin to slowly chew her cud and let out a long, low moo when she saw anyone of us even though it was three o'clock in the morning.

Will was relaxed as we headed back toward

Strawberry Hill but I could see he was full of excitement. I tried to keep up with his long, loping strides but it was no use, so he shortened them to fall back along with me.

"Hey, Annie May, what's eating you?"

"Everyone's leaving me. Carrie's made up her mind on Wells. And, Uncle John will have to hire someone to replace you because it won't be long before you're a big college man and you'll forget all about us locals in the boonies."

"How could I forget you, Annie May? Who would scold me and set me straight when I needed it?"

"Oh, quit your teasing, Will Vanderwort. I know you're going to be very busy and won't have time for Georgie or me."

"I couldn't leave Georgie just to you. Who would teach him all that man stuff?"

"Well, I know Georgie's going to miss you. He doesn't say because he keeps a lot inside, but I know he hangs his head and looks sad whenever Uncle John talks about going into town to post a notice at the new Agway for a new hired hand come September.

"Did you hear from Cornell yet?"

"That's what I was going to tell you, Annie May. The Ag school accepted me. I got my letter in the mail last Tuesday."

"Congratulations, Will," I said in a voice that sounded more like an echo, "I know you'll do well. And, they're lucky to have you."

"Thanks, Annie May. I'll write when I can and I'll tell you what it's like because you'll be going off soon yourself."

As we reached Strawberry Hill I looked for the ripest and the plumpest berries on the wild plants that were scattered about the hill. But, as always, Will was way ahead of me. As he dropped berry after berry into the pail, I saw my pie come out of the oven. I would taste the berries and add just enough sugar to add to the sweetness they already had.

"Hey, Annie May, if I pick all the berries, you're going to have to save me a piece of the pie."

"Oh, Will, you know I always save you some pie. You're the only one who can wheedle a piece of Mama's strawberry rhubarb pie without saying anything."

Although we all knew that Mama saved the choicest part of the pie for Georgie, Will ran a close second. She knew that his folks had it hard, never having lived long enough in one place to soak up the country, to be a part of it.

The sun was setting and I knew we had to get back, but I felt we could stay here forever. I stared at the sky with its broad sweeps of mauves, pale yellows, and brilliant orange-red, some of it borrowed from the arc of a beautiful, pale rainbow against a light blue sky and fluffy white clouds and the burst of sunlight after a drenching downpour.

We walked back silently, each of us lost in our very own thoughts. The moon would soon be up and it would be a new moon, a sliver. I knew the phases of the moon like I knew arithmetic and which way the rivers run.

I said goodbye to Will, promising him the best piece of pie and trying not to cross my fingers behind my back. I made a mental note to include some for Jester.

I hurried into the house. I knew Mama would need some help with supper and although it was planting time and the whiff of spring was in the air, the annual siren song for poor struggling students, I went directly to the kitchen. I knew my homework would be waiting for me after the chores were done and the last supper dish was dried and neatly stacked in the old pinewood cupboards.

Chapter Twelve

It was a beautiful spring day when Mama and I spent the morning cleaning and dusting. The windows were open and the scents of spring wafted through, the cherry blossoms hinting at the small luscious fruit they would bring, the apple blossoms the delicious smell of a newly ripened McIntosh, and the crabapple tree the memory of tart jelly spread on a freshly baked slice of sourdough on a cold winter's morning.

The chatter of men wafted in as well, their voices full of cheer as they dragged the spreader from the barn to hook onto the tractor and fertilize the new seedlings that had already sprouted up. The sun shone fully today, its rays the harbinger of hope.

"Mama, have you ever thought of marrying again?"

"Why, no, Annie May, I have not given it a thought. Your Papa was man enough for me and then some."

"The widow Perkins just married Mr. Ambler, the blacksmith who has that shop in town. I hear they had a big, old-fashioned wedding and all their kinfolk came, even those who lived two states away."

"Well, I'm not sure I could handle another man with all I have to do."

"Lucy said it was a fancy wedding with flowers all over and plenty to eat. Little tea sandwiches, barbecue chicken and salads, pies and cakes, and toasted marshmallows in the evening over a great big bonfire. They had square dancing in the afternoon, with Hallie Perkins fiddling and Dusty Perkins calling."

"It sounds like a hoot and I'm happy for Mazie Perkins but she's going to have her hands full with seven children between them."

"Lucy says they have it all fixed up. Hallie's old enough to handle the little ones, and the blacksmith business and the shop in town bring in a pretty good income."

"Hank Peterson at the dry goods store has hinted for years that he would be interested in marriage. But, all he was was at loose ends when Dorrie died, what with three kids and a store to run. I don't think I can take on that kind of work. And, besides, your papa's memory suits me fine."

I set my feather duster back into the closet in the kitchen, its feathers duly shaken in the soft, mellow outdoor air.

"You go along, Annie May. I'm going to work on that pie. I'm going to make a chocolate custard pie until we get some fruit to shake off those trees."

"I know Georgie loves your chocolate custard, Mama. He's going to find it a real treat after those men get through making him do all the gofer work."

"Uncle John does a good job looking after Georgie. I know he rides him hard, but he's trying to make a farmer out of him. And, Georgie loves the land."

"Well, Will will take up the slack where Uncle John lets off."

"Georgie adores Will, Annie May. I don't know what I would have done, with all us girls around here, and no men for Georgie to look up to. But, Will has been a lifesaver. I'm going to miss him."

I put back the vacuum and folded up the dust cloth. I gave Mama a hug.

When I heard her safely clanging the sifter and pulling the pie plates and the rolling pin out of the cupboards, I crept up the back stairway to the attic. It was time to dig into the stash of neatly stacked journals willed to us and so lovingly preserved by Granny Rosie.

The third was bound in faded red leather and contained a loose, tattered, and yellowed first page in the hand of Granny.

The following passages are taken from the memoir of Thomas Wilkes, whose many descendants include my great-grandfather Alfred Maynard Adams in direct lineage. Although the full text of Thomas Wilkes' memoir has been lost, Charity Adams, wife of Alfred, preserved the following passages in this small bound volume and has passed them down.

My name is Thomas Wilkes and I was born in the small town of Lowestoft on the eastern shore of England in 1730. At the age of seven I was taken from the quay where I was playing along the wharf and shoved into a boat by some rough and evil men. After a very stormy and rough crossing, I was taken to America and sold as an indentured servant to a plantation in Virginia. I was ill-used and suffered constant sickness and hunger. Neither scurvy or bloody flux were strangers to the many indentured servants working there, and we worked long hours every day for a mouthful of bread and sometimes bits of beef and a small amount of daily gruel. My clothes were rags, no shirt or shoes or cap, and the only cloak I had was stolen by a fellow worker who sold it for some bread down at the docks. I worked for many years like this and all around me fellows cried out they would rather be back in England without their limbs and live as beggars than live like this.

When we went to the boats to deliver and unload, we were bade to lie in the boat all night without shelter until morning and Goodman Johnson, a local man, made me a covering and his wife was kind to me and gave me comfort. He said it would rather I had been knocked over the head than sold as an indentured servant.

After a number of years like this and no sign of reprieve since the master kept finding reasons to increase the number of years of our servitude, Goodman Johnson took pity on me and helped me escape, first hiding out in the cellar of his small house, then going north to the state of New York where a friend of his was looking for an apprentice to his printing company. I was given a suit of clothes so as not to be noticed and I was told how to travel by night and how to travel by the north star. I was given a small compass and food to last and the knowledge of how to catch fish should I come upon a lake or river. I also had a trap which I could use if I was near a woodland and a gun for my protection.

I reached Albany County in the state of New York where Josiah Alexander, the friend of Goodman Johnson, lived. He was happy to see me and he and his wife Mary welcomed me warmly and immediately gave me shelter. He was an established printer and as such offered me an apprenticeship which would give me room and board and the opportunity to learn a trade. I accepted with gratitude.

As I understood it, the house had been lonely before my arrival. Josiah and Mary Alexander had been the parents of six children, two who died in infancy, and four who were lost to either tuberculosis or rheumatic fever. Although both Josiah and Mary were both strict Baptist fundamentalists and attended church every Sunday where I was bade to go as well, and although they did not allow playing cards or dancing, there was much that was pleasant in their house. Our evening meals were bountiful and Mary spent the day baking the most delicious bread, pulling from her cast-iron oven the most mouth-watering pies, and the aroma of her stews and soups often drifted from her kitchen to the print shop out back.

It was at the age of sixteen that I was given the offer to remain in Josiah's printing business and receive a very small salary or to go off on my own with a small sum that Josiah could afford to part with. I chose to stay and save the money I earned as a stake toward a print shop of my own. I left Josiah and Mary's small farm at the age of eighteen and set up shop in the nearby small town of Lufton. I chose that location rather than strike out for the west to seek my fortune because I knew Josiah and Mary would need looking after in their old age.

I found a room in town over the general store and settled in there while I opened a print shop. Life in Lufton was very different from the life on the Alexander homestead. It was filled with gaiety and constant bustle, what with townsfolk and farmers coming in daily for supplies, chatter on the sidewalks, and fights in the saloon after dark.

I kept to myself and opened my print shop which was soon thriving due to the arrival of merchants anxious to open shops free of the competition of bigger cities and due to the political climate of neighboring metropolises.

When I was about a year with my print shop a woman who was about the best looking I had ever seen entered my shop. She was there to purchase labels for her father's herbal medicine shop. Since he had developed business in far flung places about the country and had to ship to those places he also needed a constant supply of shipping labels and labels for the many bottles he kept on his shelves. We struck up a lively conversation and recognizing that I was alone in my living arrangements started bringing me occasional pots of the most delicious stews and sometimes a peach or apple pie.

She was a kind woman and her long dark hair which fell beneath her bonnet seemed to match the gaiety in her face and the sparkle in her eyes which were as clear and blue as the prized agates the village lads rolled about as shooters in their zeal to win at a game of marbles. I took to getting a length of satin ribbon down at the general store so that when she came in I could give her a present when she brought me a pie or a slice of fresh baked bread.

It was soon that I realized that she would make a perfect wife but I wasn't sure if she would have me or if her father would give his consent. After all, I was nothing, an indentured servant and apprentice and it is true, a successful print shop owner, but I was fearful my severe background would be held against me.

I asked permission to court her from her father and he hesitatingly gave his consent. Although he was wary of me, he very much wanted to please his only daughter, and Abigail, as she was called, was sweet on me as I was on her.

After a year of courtship, her father gave his consent and we were married in the church outside of town. Josiah and Mary were there dressed in their Sunday best and beaming with happiness for me. Their wedding gift was a sack of flour and one of meal and a beautiful pinewood chair Josiah had turned himself. I was never so happy as when we drove away in the buggy Abigail's father had lent us for the occasion.

We soon settled down on a parcel of land Abigail's father gave us outright since he was comfortable and had prospered through the years in his business. It being outside of town and a pretty good sized spread, we were able to farm the land and provide a bounty of food for the little ones who came along after our marriage.

Our family grew and our small farm prospered as did the print shop. We were able to add a large barn on our farm for two cows and a few goats and set up a small creamery. As our sons grew they apprenticed in the print shop to learn the trade. They were even able to attend the school that Abigail set up in a small log building behind our barn.

But, despite our good fortune and the gaiety and happy times we shared, there was something that I felt missing since I landed on the soil of this country. I had every day wondered about my mother and my father and the little ones who came after me since I was the eldest. I was certain that they never would have sold me into servitude.

I felt that if I was to get any rest at all inside of me I must find the truth. I laid my plan before Abigail and she being the loving companion that she was understood my need.

I set sail for England not long after and left my family in the care of Josiah and Mary Alexander. Abigail's father looked in on them often since although he had in the beginning some objections to me he had grown very fond of his grandchildren and often spoiled them despite our protests.

I arrived in England in what was the cold and rainy season. I embarked in London and traveled to Lowestoft on foot and sometimes by carriage or buggy if I was fortunate enough to find a willing stranger sympathetic to my plight. I arrived in Lowestoft in the span of one month.

My questions to the many villagers I met yielded no information on my parents or my younger brothers or sisters. But, there was an informant who had been wronged by the magistrates of the village who was hasty to tell me what he knew about the trade of selling unsuspecting children into servitude. It was the magistrates, he told me, who had been charged with upholding the law of the village who had collected large sums of money from traders looking for a profit by kidnapping children who had wandered from their homes and were playing about the environs of the village.

I set about to bring suit against the magistrates for the crime of my kidnapping. But, on the day of the court hearing, they brought in as judge one of the very magistrates that had helped to arrange my kidnapping. He ruled against me and of course I lost.

Discouraged, I turned to a constable in the next town over who advised me to take the case and the hearing to the city of Blenheim where a higher court would be disposed to rule more fairly. I won and was compensated with a good deal of money which I used to search for the whereabouts of my parents and sisters and brothers.

A very large bribe brought information from a former magistrate who knew about a letter that concerned me and had been left with the clergyman of the local church. Not knowing who I was when I had arrived, or hearing about my appearance, he had not stepped forward. It took much persuasion and a large donation to retrieve the letter but he finally pulled it from the very dusty archives in the lowest basement of the manor house.

It was an eerie feeling to find such a letter which had yellowed with age but despite my trembling I pulled it from its sealed envelope and began to read.

Dear Thomas,

My dear eldest and loving son.

We have given up hope of ever finding you but we pray for you every day.

You have seven brothers and sisters now and that makes many mouths to feed. Your father has done his best to provide for us but he is saddened that he has no eldest son to help him ply his trade. He can no longer be a smithy since he was put into debtors prison and crushed his hand wielding a pickaxe on the rock pile. He finds metal scraps and sells them, and I take in laundry and sometimes sewing, but it is never enough.

We have survived the last famine but the fever has taken our two littlest ones from us.

We have thought that you might have been taken with the child trade that no one will confess to but we have heard of through the starving and tattered men who live around the docks and forage for the fish that slip through the nets of the fishermen.

If you have been taken, my son, we can only hope that it is a better life you have gone to and that your lot will be better than it could be here.

We have loved you from the day you were born and came into our lives, a happy little baby who knew so much laughter.

If by some good chance you will someday come upon this letter, then know how much we love you and wish for your good fortune.

Your loving mother,
Emmaline Wilkes

I was very distraught that I could not find news of my family's whereabouts. The clergyman was no help since he had received the letter for safekeeping from a villager who no longer lived there. But, after asking about town in many quarters I finally came upon the letter bearer's whereabouts and tracked him to a nearby town.

The man was glad to see me and told me all he could. He had been a long time neighbor of my family and as such had been a comfort to them as they were to him. When the fever hit, my family had all been wiped out. This man, whose name was Jonathan Sprigs, cared for them until the end, and was spared the scourge which affected a large number in the village.

Mr. Sprigs told me of my family's last days. He nursed them as best he could. My mother, who could not read or write, asked him to write a letter for her and made him promise that he would put it in the hands of the church for safekeeping which he faithfully obliged. He then buried my mother and my father and my brothers and sisters who had all been struck down by the fever in the public cemetery.

I thanked him for his care and for relating to me their circumstances. I then left him with a good amount of the sum of money I had left because I could see he could use it. I then set off for the Lowestoft public cemetery.

There were no markers but Mr. Sprigs had identified each plot with a simple iron plate which he had inscribed himself. I commissioned the stonemason in the village to craft markers for each of the graves my family occupied and gave a sum of money to a young maiden in the village to look after them for me when I was gone. She promised to plant white lilies which had been my mother's favorite flower since she had seen them in church as a girl.

I left Lowestoft with a heavy heart and with the letter my mother had written. But, I was anxious to return to my home since it had been long since I had been gone and I knew by now the crops would need tending and the print shop, though in the capable hands of Josiah, would need that extra hand. And, I feared by now Abigail would find a need to enlist my help to keep the little ones out of mischief.

I returned home to a joyful reunion. I showed Abigail the letter that had been written by my mother and she placed it alongside the family bible for safekeeping.

When I returned to my print shop I started a post office for the merchants in town. It was soon that the merchants in neighboring towns traveled to Lufton to make use of it. Many were now able to ship to the Continent and we became a thriving center for international trade.

> Respectfully submitted in the year
> 1763 by
> Thomas Wilkes

I closed the slim journal gently so as not to disrupt the aging papers.

Granny had always been a tower of strength to me. But, now it was clear that she had a long line of forbears to call on when the going got rough as she bustled about, feather duster in hand, or kept the house cats from getting trampled in the rough housing that was inevitable after a Sunday dinner.

I felt a rush of pride as I realized these were my ancestors too. I would conquer the world and make them proud. They had sacrificed and survived so I could have a better life.

But how could a simple farm girl like me make a difference? I decided to shelve the thought and head toward my pile of unfinished homework. As I went, the aroma of chocolate custard pie baking in the oven wafted up the old stairwell along with a rush of soft spring air drifting in from the open windows.

Chapter Thirteen

C arrie's graduation fell on a very rainy day. All hopes of an outdoor ceremony disappeared as I peered out the windows in the very early morning to see a dark and cloudy gray sky with buckets of water pouring down and flooding the cistern.

Carrie had been up for hours. She had been practicing the very short acceptance speech she had written for the honor of being chosen the best girl artist in her senior class. Brent Armstrong, an acne-ridden slight boy with thin, brownish hair had been chosen best boy artist.

Carrie had not considered pursuing art. Her main interest in school had been boys. But, she was nevertheless flattered by the award and had spent long hours writing her acceptance speech and begging me to polish it for her.

She looked beautiful as always as she dressed for the very important occasion. But, I couldn't help sensing a wistful look as she placed her best brooch, a pearl and gem-studded rabbit, on the collar of her simple linen dress that was belted and pleated in the softest lilac hue. Her long dark hair was unbound and hanging free about her shoulders. Carrie would be a stunner as usual, but I could see her mind wasn't on that.

"What's up, Squirrel?" I said, bringing her back to the moment.

"I don't know, Annie May. I should be happy. But, I'm full of worry. I'll be losing Jamie to Harvard and a bunch of really smart girls to chase after him. I'm not sure how I'll take to staying on campus. I know I'll like the girls at Wells. I met some of them at the open house. But, I'll miss the life we've had here. Some of those girls are so sophisticated and I'm not sure I'll measure up."

"Carrie, you're the most beautiful girl I've ever seen and one of the most caring. There should be plenty of girls to appreciate that there. And, if they don't, they don't belong knowing you.

"As for Jamie, I've seen him look at you. I don't think Jamie's the type to have his head turned by glitter.

"You won't be far from here. And, I know Georgie will be begging me to bring him there to visit. He always needs your input for his art projects. And, you know Mama will insist on tucking in some oatmeal raisin cookies because she knows they're your favorite."

Carrie gave me a hug. "Annie May, you're the best."

I knew I hadn't completely set Carrie's mind at ease. But, every now and then I could take the edge off.

As I stood wondering how I would get my own pale lime linen over my head with the zipper set too short a frantic Georgie burst into our room unannounced to stand in front of Carrie. "Carrie, can you tie this tie?"

Carrie looked at the newly purchased string tie all knotted in Georgie's hand and tried hard not to laugh. I had to hand it to Mama. Hank Peterson down at the dry goods store could talk Mama into anything.

"Georgie, let's see. I think we can make something really fashionable out of it."

"Aw, Carrie, I just hope none of the kids laugh at me. I never saw a tie like this."

"They're all the rage in New York. The western look has really caught on in the big cities. Why, Georgie, you're going to be the handsomest brother at the graduation."

I could see Georgie was unconvinced, but stood patiently while Carrie tried to make sense out of a long, narrow piece of double grosgrain fabric. As she began turning the fabric under the collar of Georgie's best white shirt, Mama burst into the room, already decked out in a beautiful floral silk. I could see she was about to hurry us along but stopped short of rushing us as she stared at the black grosgrain now being turned into a handsomely tied bow.

"Papa used to favor a tie like that," she said. "Why, when it was in fashion he was the talk of all the socials for his smart dress.

Papa would be so proud of you, Carolyn Ann. I know he would. But, we're all proud of you. You will be the first of our family to go to college. It's quite an achievement. I know that if Granny and Gramps were here they would be so puffed up with pride they could burst."

I didn't want to mention that if I hadn't done most of Carrie's homework while she was busy mooning over boys she might not have gotten into Wells. But, I thought it best to let Carrie have her day since she did try to bring a certain amount of sunlight into what might have otherwise been a pretty ordinary existence.

"Okay, let's get hurrying," Mama cautioned, as she swished out of the room, the silk of her calf-length flounces rustling as she walked. "Uncle John and Aunt Mabel will be here soon. And, you know how Aunt Mabel doesn't like to wait."

My lime green linen gave me a certain amount of trouble but Carrie saved the day by finally getting it over my head and letting gravity do the rest. As she stood back to survey the final result, she shook her head and reached into her special scarf drawer, a small drawer neatly lined with floral scented paper and filled with color coded squares and rectangles, florals which Carrie favored, some geometrics and solids. She quickly pulled out a long rectangular silk with every shade of green inked into its pattern of leaves, trees, and imaginary elves. She tied it around my waist and stood back, admiring her work and satisfied that I was now complete.

"Annie May, you are going to be the hit of the outgoing junior class."

Since I wasn't the preening type, I was quite taken with the assessment. I only hoped that Jason Harper, a boy I had had my eye on since third grade, would notice.

Uncle John and Aunt Mabel arrived all spruced up with Uncle John's pickup newly washed and waxed.

Aunt Mabel's freshly permed hair was rinsed with the henna she favored, and her navy linen with matching jacket would be sure to get notice from her garden club associates who passed for society in these parts and who showed up in full force every year at graduation to accept their certificate for spending every spring and fall planting and cultivating, tulips and daffodils in the spring, chrysanthemums and asters in the fall, to beautify the school grounds.

We arrived at the school without incident. The heavy rains had let up and were replaced with a beautiful mist and a rainbow up above us, its pale hues against the brightening sky unnoticed by the crowd bent on making haste to secure the more favored center seating in the newly refurbished auditorium. I silently placed it on my list of so far unused omens and tried to keep up with Mama and Aunt Mabel who were nodding to all their acquaintances as they rushed.

Carrie left us to seat herself in the special section reserved for graduates and the rest of us settled in the rows of attached faux leather seats which still smelled new and that replaced the familiar, old wooden folding chairs purchased years ago with the proceeds of a particularly successful bake sale. The auditorium had been transformed, the school banner hung behind a microphone and lectern up on the stage, and the spot behind it where our principal Mr. Andrews would hand out the diplomas was flanked by two large urns filled with the most beautiful flowers, both vivid and pale, arranged to bring out the hues of the summer so nearly upon us.

I scanned the graduates for Will. His blond good looks stood out and I spotted him seated next to Carrie. As I tried to get his attention without success Mr. Andrews strode to the podium and a collective hush took over.

"Good morning graduates, parents, relatives, and friends. I am happy to be presiding over the 45th Baldwinsville Central School District commencement ceremony. I know we all share a collective pride in our graduates. We will begin the formal part of our program with the pledge of allegiance followed by our alma mater led by Mrs. Regina Carter, our notable music liaison who took the chorus to the semi-finals this year. Please all rise."

Chapter Fourteen

The alma mater, its words penned to a popular ballad of the day by a former Baldwinsville student now long gone from these beige and whitewashed halls, rang from the rafters of the auditorium with the gusto of the former students now singing it. We sat as one as the final chorus came to a rousing end.

Mr. Andrews rose to announce the awards and bring the recipients to the stage. The first was Ida Harper, the president of the Mayberry Garden Club, who would be presented with a plaque by Mrs. Alma Hutchinson, our perennially grim but excellent biology teacher, who appeared from the wings of the stage with a beautifully carved wooden plaque made by the shop class and lettered in gold.

As we waited for Mrs. Harper, flushed with excitement and dressed in a deep purple linen suit with an American Beauty rosebud attached securely to her lapel, to pass by the people she was seated with and make her way up the stairs to the podium I realized that not only Carrie would be giving a speech,

Will would be giving one too. In a surprise upset, Will had surpassed Jackson Monroe III who was known mostly as "Junior", and the odds on favorite to become valedictorian, by a mere two tenths of a point, throwing the Monroe family into a snit to have their star pupil knocked out by someone they considered an immigrant upstart. The Monroe family, the only family we could claim in these parts had come from "wealth," had refrained from sending their only child to a private school in Syracuse, or away to boarding school where the competition was truly stiff, so that he could excel in a school they were certain was populated only by country bumpkins.

Mrs. Harper made it to the stage without incident and Mrs. Hutchinson presented the plaque as ceremoniously as she could, giving a partial history of the garden club and regaling the audience with their contributions to the school and to the town. The yearbook photographer knelt as quietly as he could on the auditorium floor at the foot of the stage to commemorate the presentation. Mr. Harper rushed to the aisle of his row to snap a photograph, catching Mrs. Harper as she grasped the plaque and held it, exchanging a handshake with Mrs. Hutchinson who seemed anxious to end the presentation and exit the stage.

Mr. Andrews continued the presentations and it wasn't long before Carrie's name was called. "Caroline Ann Parker, winner of the best girl artist award, would you please come to the stage to receive your certificate?"

Carrie rushed past all in her row to reach the aisle and change her gait to one of extreme decorum. Her posture as she climbed the few stairs to reach the stage was one of perfect alignment and her carriage oozed the grace of one who had practiced this many times over.

"Caroline Ann, you have been voted best girl artist by your classmates. May you put your talent to good use in your future. Congratulations."

Carrie shook hands with Mr. Andrews with the most grace I had seen in her in a long time. I could see her hands shaking as she took the certificate and I could feel her pride as Mr. Andrews seated himself in the folding chair behind the lectern.

Carrie stepped forward and adjusted the microphone.

"To my classmates who voted me this honor, I

thank you for your support and hope I will justify your belief in me. To our valued teachers, especially Mrs. Turner, my art teacher for three years, I would like to express my deepest gratitude for all your encouragement, patience, and the very best art supplies.

"Most of all, I would like to thank my family for putting up with years of canvases and finger paints without complaint.

"I would like to add my congratulations to my fellow graduates and wish them the best that the future holds. Thank you."

Carrie left the stage and reseated herself next to Will. Mr. Andrews introduced the remaining awards and scholarships and then turned the podium over to Ted Parsons, the most popular boy in school and president of his class for the last three years. His speech, though short and modest, was the most polished we had heard, and we were certain he was headed for a brilliant future.

As Ted returned to his seat amidst an admiring round of applause, Mr. Andrews rose to announce the valedictorian. A hush took over and mutterings were heard through the large Monroe clan, complete with relatives who had traveled from mainline Philadelphia and the suburbs of Long Island.

"Will Vanderwort has achieved the honor of class valedictorian with a grade point average of 96.5. Will, please come up and address your classmates."

Will strode to the stage, unruffled by the more audible foot shufflings and grumblings of the Monroe clan, and reached the lectern to shake hands with Mr. Andrews. He placed his neatly folded notes on its slanted top as Mr. Andrews reseated himself and began.

"Parents, faculty, and fellow students, I thank you for this honor.

"I know that I have achieved this by hard work, but no one achieves anything alone. I would like to thank my parents who have always been supportive of my endeavors. I would also like to thank Mr. John Turner, and the Parker family, who hired me on as a farm worker when I was new to the community and had no farm experience at all, teaching me not only about farm work but about humility and generosity. To my fellow students who reached out to me with friendship when I was a new arrival I extend my gratitude and would like you to know how much I value your friendship. And to Mr. Andrews, who helped me fit in when I arrived, and to the teachers of Baldwinsville who worked every day to teach me everything they know, I extend my earnest gratitude as well.

"Everyone in this graduating class has a talent for something. I would urge my fellow classmates to guard those talents and to use them in some way to better the world. It seems to me the duty of anyone who has been given as much as we have.

"I can't forget the times we hung out together at the swimming holes or occasionally cut up in town and got into mischief. I hope we don't forget those times as well, because it will help us to remember where we come from and the responsibilities we face as new graduates.

"I again thank you all for this honor and wish the very best of luck and good fortune to my fellow classmates.

"Thank you."

As Will finished, Mr. Andrews stepped up to the podium to hand Will his diploma, asking him to remain on the stage as he passed out the diplomas. Miss Ames, Baldwinsville's office secretary since the opening of the school, stepped up as well, a stack of diplomas in hand, all alphabetized and ready to hand to Mr. Andrews as he called out the formal names of the graduates in a loud, clear voice, asking the audience to hold their applause until the last student had their diploma in their possession.

Mr. Andrews shook every graduate's hand as he handed them their diploma and as each one left the stage I felt a surge of pride even though I didn't know most of the Mayberry students. Somehow, despite the fact that many of them felt superior to us farm folk, they were starting on a path that was not only unknown, a lot was expected of them. To me, soon to be a senior myself, it was all very frightening, and certainly very humbling.

Mr. Andrews then gave a speech himself, again congratulating the class of 1954 and urging them to take what they have learned and make their mark in the world and on humanity. He also urged them to take risks and not be afraid to fail. Edison, he reminded them, completed hundreds of failed experiments before he found the one that invented the light bulb. He then invited everyone to a reception of punch and cookies, cakes and homemade candies to be held following the ceremony in the gymnasium newly decorated for the occasion by the Art Club.

As Mr. Andrews announced a conclusion to the ceremony, screams of joy erupted from the graduates, and confetti and crepe paper streamers were everywhere. Plans were made for beer blasts and families searched for their graduate to congratulate them. I spotted Carrie, hugging her classmates for perhaps the very last time. Will searched for his parents, their beaming faces glowing in the crowd. As for me, I stood, overlooked by everybody, waiting for the crowd to disperse so we could follow the whitewashed halls to the gymnasium, its bland ropes and sports equipment pushed to the side in favor of gaily-colored balloons, many now disrupted by unthinking celebrants and rising to the rafters of the mile-high two-storied ceiling to be perhaps unnoticed forever.

Chapter Fifteen

Carrie's graduation party was filled with relatives from as far away as Texas since it was our turn to host the biennial family reunion. Aunt Maybelle arrived with her clan to help Mama with the fixings and the trimmings and Uncle Elbert arrived to dig a pit in the backyard for barbecue and marshmallows.

Mama baked her prize-winning cherry pie and Aunt Maybelle her strawberry rhubarb which had won a blue ribbon in the Ohio State Fair. Carrie and I made little tea sandwiches for days before the party and froze them. Georgie helped Uncle Elbert dig the backyard pit and clear the barn for square dancing.

The day of the party brought the sunniest weather ever, driving some of the guests inside to seek relief from the many fans Mama had set up and to exchange the gossip they had kept since the last reunion in Ohio. As for the rest of us, we were kept busy refilling the plates of barbecued chicken and ribs and replenishing the salads and slaws that were so quickly disappearing. Children were set up in the back field with rented swings and slides and a pony our neighbor Jeb Taylor had lent us for the occasion. Georgie held sway over the pony rides and set up pails for berry picking as well.

Kegs of beer laid low the fiddling contest which was held in the barn and which was a draw between Texas and New York. Square dancing soon replaced it, with Zack Turner taking a turn at calling and a slightly tipsy fiddler backing him up. The reds and the blues and the greens of swirling skirts made a colorful canvas against the old, brown, rotting timbers holding up the walls of the ancient barn.

"Annie May, the potato salad bowls need filling and the popsicles need to be carted out to the back for the little ones. It's getting to be nap time."

Mama's firm, clear voice above the hubbub where she was holding sway in the kitchen brought me back to reality and into the kitchen to fetch the large pots of salads and find the red wagon which had been pressed into service for transportation from the deep freeze to the back fields where an exhausted Georgie watched over a passel of tired, cranky toddlers.

"Hey, Annie May, let me help you with those." As I turned, Will had already snatched the large pot of potato salad from the fairly loose hold I had on it and into his sure and steady grip. I wasn't about to let on that my arms were aching so I smiled a funny smile and mumbled the best few words of gratitude I could muster.

"How about sneaking out to Strawberry Hill? We could take a spin in the barn and then out past the crowd."

"Okay. Let's get this potato salad out before there's mutiny in the kitchen."

As Will and I strolled toward the barn I realized a crowd this size must be overwhelming to someone who has no relatives in America. I hurried my step to keep up. We reached the barn just as Zack began calling a reel I had never heard of. We took our places and Will did a fine step for someone whose heritage was far from country.

As we left, the sun began to lower in the sky and the cloying heat of noontime was cooling. The little ones would be put in for a nap by now and the beer drinkers would be safely in their tents or RV's for a nap as well. Relative quiet would be descending and the women would be catching up on gossip as they wiped and dried and set out platters for the evening meal.

The summer air, though heavy and humid, carried the odor of fertilizer and the scent of soil giving birth to the corn and the beans and the pea pods Uncle John and Will and Georgie had planted in the spring. The orchards had sprouted their blossoms and the cherry trees had already borne fruit.

Will was scanning the fields. "Crops look great. I'll miss harvest this year."

"Oh, you'll be so busy hitting the books you won't even notice."

"I'll notice, Annie May. Farming's in my genes, even though I don't come from a long line of farmers like you do. But, I want to contribute in a different way. I'll be learning all the new advances and all the research that promises a better future for farming. And, if I can get into vet school I can help in a different way."

"And, then, you'll be able to help all those strays you keep taking in."

"Well that will be part of it. I hope I can help to get rid of some of those diseases that wipe out farmers."

As for me, I just wanted to hang on to this moment. As we walked through the meadows rife with the tall summer grasses both golden and green and the wild flowers interspersed among them, the pale soft hue of the bluebells, the brilliant orange of the lilies, and the always lovely yellows and whites of the daisies, I breathed deeply of the mellow and lovely scented summer air.

As we reached the bottom of Strawberry Hill, Will paused. "I've climbed this hill hundreds of times in all kinds of weather, but somehow this time just seems so special."

"Oh, for gosh sakes, Will Vanderwort, you're not leaving forever. You'll be back on vacations and I know you'll have your hand in tending the crops over the summer no matter how busy you are. This farm couldn't get along without you."

"I'd like to think that, Annie May. But, your Uncle John is a fine farmer and can get along with just about any hired hand."

"He'll miss you, Will. I know he will. But, he is so proud of you. Especially since you've chosen to study agriculture. He almost feels like he had a hand in that."

"He might have had. I always wanted to contribute to the world. What better way is there than to help feed it? Especially to help men as devoted as your Uncle John."

"C'mon, I'll race you to the top."

Will's long bounds could take me, but he let me win. A parting gift and a nod to his growing maturity. I stood atop the rise in triumph.

As we stood we surveyed the bumper crop of wild, plump berries. Beautiful nestled in the greenery of the saw-toothed stark foliage. We plopped ourselves down, out of breath, on the very top.

Will pulled a small package out of his pocket. "I have made this for you, Annie May."

I opened the carefully wrapped box and pulled out what looked to be a wild boar with a golden mane. I was mystified, but also speechless. Will took over.

"It's a likeness of Gullinbursti, the favored steed of the Norse god Freyr. Gullinbursti is said to travel faster than a horse or bird. His golden mane and bristles can light the skies more brightly than the sun.

"He is said to have been created by two dwarf brothers who were told they could not outdo the gifts that had already been presented to Odin, the chief

Norse god. Despite setbacks and attempts to sabotage their efforts, they fired up their forge and created a wild boar with golden mane and bristles that Odin prized above all other gifts.

"Gullinbursti has helped farmers since he was created. His tusks can plow the entire Earth. He has the knowledge to make plants sprout and flourish. His golden bristles light up the skies when they are grey.

"My Dutch ancestors put a lot of faith in Gullinbursti when the going got rough. I want you to keep him for me. He will watch over the farm when I am gone. And, I know you will be doing that too. I know Georgie will depend on you now and the rest of your family as well even though they won't let on that that's what they're doing.

"It has meant a lot for me to know you and your family, Annie May. They took me in on faith when I first arrived and never questioned me since."

""Well, you know you've repaid them. Georgie adores you, and Mama would spoil you almost as much as Georgie if anyone would let her."

"What are your plans, Annie May? What will you do when we're all in college?"

"I want to be a teacher. I want to teach children

about all the books we have in that library over in town and open up a whole new world to them. Those books were my salvation when the going got rough here."

"I know you'll make it, Annie May. You're smart and you've got grit."

"Thanks, Will. I know I can beat any boy in rounding up the livestock or stray horses or pigs.

"I guess we should get back. Mama's going to wonder where I am. She needs all the help she can get to feed this crowd."

Will and I walked back, the sun lowering in the sky behind us. We walked in silence, the only sound the birds chattering in the nearby orchards. When we returned, Will put himself to work with Georgie and Uncle Elbert to finish off the backyard pit and find appropriate spits for the marshmallow roast. The square dancing had ended, Zack was begging food in the kitchen, and the fiddler was asleep in the corner of the barn beneath the hayloft.

The night was beautiful under the stars. As we sang beneath the darkened sky, and roasted piles of marshmallows, our faces were lit by the flames of the open pit. Suddenly we were one. Our voices carried to the hills beyond and the chirping of crickets filled the silence between the old, familiar tunes. I searched for the outlines of the distant peaks, barely visible in the moonlight, and basked in the cooling breeze coming in to cast a slight chill over the warmth of a musky summer evening.

Chapter Sixteen

As the sun streamed into the kitchen with its shadows behind it getting ready to set with the reds of an evening sky Georgie picked at his food and Mama and I discussed the latest autumn fashions. Setting three places at supper only made it clearer that Carrie was at Wells.

"Hey, Georgie," I said, "how about us making a leather bag for Carrie to carry her books in?"

"Could we make one for Will too?"

"Of course. Two bags are better than one because that way we'll get really good at it."

"Could we make something for Jester too? Will said I should look in on him and make sure he's okay while he's away."

"Well, I think Jester will be happy if we make him some treats. We can bake him some beef bones with the leftover pot roast Mama's so good at making."

Georgie's eating picked up and Mama and I decided that the plaids that were in this year were perfect for the sweaters she had knitted last year. After much discussion, she decided on a cable knit for Carrie which was much the new fashion at Hank Peterson's dry goods store and a pair of argyle socks for Georgie to bring his Sunday suit in line with the latest New York fashions according to the fall Sears catalog which Mama believed was gospel.

"Okay, Georgie, last one up with their plate washes."

"Now, Anabel May, we don't need any broken crockery to sweep up. Besides, you know it's your turn to wash."

"Okay, Georgie wins. And, if you get a head start on your homework I'll leave the dishes to drain and we can both put them up in the cupboard together."

"Do you promise, Annie May? Mr. Thompson gave us so much math homework and it's hard this year."

"You work on it while I wash the dishes and I'll go over it with you after you're done."

"Thanks, Annie May. I hope I get it right."

"You get it as right as you can and then we'll figure it out together."

Georgie headed upstairs and Mama to the alcove off the dining room that held her faithful sewing machine that had been in her family before her. Although there were newer models on the market, Mama swore by that old treadle which she had named Bessie, alternately encouraging it and fussing at it depending on whether it needed a squirt of oil, a bobbin changed, or was just plain running out of steam.

Helping Georgie with his math homework was more than difficult. It was downright near impossible. Georgie had no interest in figuring anything, whether it was the area of an octagon or whether a group of girl scouts would beat a group of boy scouts to the finish line based on how fast each one was paddling a canoe.

But, Georgie did try. He wanted to make Mama proud, especially to fill the void that Carrie's departure had left. We all missed Carrie, but Georgie especially had been her favorite.

"What color do you want the book bags for Carrie and Will to be?"

"Gee, Annie May, what color do you think they'll like?"

"I just saw a new bolt of leather come in at the dry goods store. Mr. Peterson says it's the latest shade. He says it's the color of a chestnut horse, all reddish-brown. It should remind Carrie of the beautiful chestnut roan she used to ride down at the Taylor farm and the chestnuts we roast together on Christmas eve."

"Maybe it'll get her to think what she's going to make me for Christmas."

"She won't forget, Georgie. Even though she's away for a while, she won't be forgetting us."

Georgie pulled from his drawer every tool he had to fashion the bag with. An awl for the grommet holes, a sharp blade to scroll the initials, a cutting tool for the pattern pieces which he would make, and a large heavy needle that would take a fine leather.

"I think we'll make this a project for tomorrow. Right now it's time for bed."

"Okay, Annie May. Sometimes, when Carrie had time she would draw me a picture."

"Well, I don't think I could do that. But, maybe we could make up a story together."

"I'll go down and put away the dishes while you get ready for bed."

"I'll be ready in no time. Almost as fast as Superman can fly."

"Okay, I'll be counting the seconds."

Mama was still fussing at Bessie as I put away the old flowered crockery that she had refused to part with because it had been Papa's favorite. As I climbed the stairs to Georgie's room, I contemplated my own nightly fate. My own room now that Carrie was at Wells. But, there was no one to share the gossip with. And, despite Carrie's petulant ways, there was no one who could create drama and speculation with so little to go on except the insistent rumors flying about over classmates and townsfolk.

Georgie was in bed with his favorite cowboy pajamas glad to be away from the math. I began my story which I was forced to make up on the spot.

"Once upon a time."

"Gee, Annie May, that's kid stuff."

"Not really, Georgie. There always will be a once upon a time."

"Okay, what's next."

"Well, once there was a boy who hated math but loved to farm. He had a mop of thick brown hair and a pair of heavy overalls which he wore when he helped to sow the seed that would grow his crops. What happens next?"

"He grows cabbages and sells them at the market. He sells more than every other farmer and he wins a prize for his cabbages at the New York State Fair."

"Well, that sounds like a good ending. Maybe we could add that he grows up and meets a beautiful girl who is like a fairy queen and together they plant crops that outgrow all the other farms in the county."

"I don't think a girl could do that. Girls are too different. They wear bows in their hair and giggle a lot."

"Carrie and I are girls, and I can outfarm any boy I choose to."

"You're different from the other girls, Annie May. And, Carrie is too. She's smart."

"I bet you have a lot of smart girls in your class but they're probably too shy to show it."

"I don't know, Annie May. Patty Masefield sits across from me and she's not so shy. She bothers me all the time. She's always throwing things at me and asking me questions."

"Well, maybe she likes you, Georgie.

"Maybe when you get to high school you'll think differently about it."

"I don't think so. Girls can't do much."

"Well, it's time to put the lights out. I'll tuck you in."

As I turned the lights out and tucked Georgie in I

bent down to kiss him goodnight but he was already asleep. I tiptoed out, bent on having a good heart to heart with Mama. Mr. Peterson had been begging me to come in on Saturdays to his dry goods store and I was anxious to see if Mama could spare me. It was a good way to save money for college and a good way to turn the talk to my own future.

As I walked softly down the old, creaky stairs the open window above the stairwell let in the starlight that streamed in to light up the old, worn carpet that barely covered the treads and the crocheted cover of the three-legged stool forever perched on the landing, its faded hues no longer drab but beautiful in the moonlight.

Chapter Seventeen

As I climbed the attic stairs to rummage about for Carrie's beautiful clay Dutch girl, a Christmas gift from Aunt Maybelle that Carrie had preserved in special paper and stored away to keep it from our occasional rough housing, and which she had now decided she could not live without because it was a perfect model for her sculpture class, I thought of the best route to take to Wells. The thruway was boring with Georgie constantly asking when we would get there, but the back roads seemed to take forever and only increased his anxiety. I decided on the thruway with more games that I could find by rummaging through the dusty piles of discarded and forgotten items nearly in front of me.

Georgie looked forward to the trips we were able to take to visit Carrie. Our old truck often barely made it, but Mama promised a new one as soon as her knit goods took off which Hank Peterson had gladly taken on commission to please Mama since he had taken a shine to her a number of years ago.

I rummaged around and found Carrie's Dutch girl easily. But, as I did the pile of journals still bound by its beautiful red bow and lying so neatly under Mama's wedding dress called to me as if they had a voice I knew they didn't possess. I settled next to them cross-legged on the old attic floor, untied the bow, and pulled out the fourth volume blowing hard to clear its dusty cover, uncovering a label that read "Papa's great-great uncle Jeremiah Reed." Inside was a note in Granny's unmistakable hand.

The following diary was sent to Patience Reed Jogger, a poor farmer's wife in Pelham, Massachusetts, from her brother Jeremiah for safe-keeping which she had kept in hiding, its whereabouts known only to her brothers and sisters and to be passed on to her eldest daughter Mary of whom Papa is a direct descendant.

I sit here gazing at the stars and writing by the moonlight. I have little time to add to this diary except at night when it is hard to labor without light to steady the way.

I write this account so my children will know

what came before them. We have great fortune here but it was not always thus.

I am grateful for what has been bestowed upon us for I am a fugitive from the state of Massachusetts with a price still on my head and have narrowly escaped hanging leaving in the dark of night for I did not know where but crossed the Massachusetts state line to Vermont and then to this vast wilderness which is part of the state of New York.

I am considered to have committed treason by a country I fought for and love.

I was a poor farmer in Massachusetts when the call for liberty came in 1776. I joined the Continental Army to fight the British and free these colonies from their steady oppression. I left our small farm where my wife Phoebe and I had barely been able to scratch out a living for ourselves and our young family, Josiah who was seven, Mary who was four and Patience who was an infant. But, we were happy and spent many an evening while Phoebe rocked our infant to sleep and we listened to the crickets in the still of a summer evening as the moonlight came through the open windows.

I fought the British and many times went without the pay we were promised but I fought because I believed in the cause of freedom from oppression. I sent whatever I could to Phoebe to keep her and the children warm and provide the means for seeds to farm our small plot of land.

Ma and Pa and especially Luke his being the eldest brother looked after Phoebe and our small family and it gave me quite a bit of security knowing they were as well cared for as could   be. Phoebe is a plucky woman and vowed to survive for the sake of the children and for my poor life as well.

I distinguished myself well as a soldier and was wounded only twice in the seven years I participated in the conflict. I was wounded once when General Howe's army routed us out of New York and once when General Washington marched us into Philadelphia and the British again were superior and wounded many and took 3,000 prisoners from which I was lucky to escape.

I fought alongside many men who were

conscripted to the cause and believed in it or were fighting for promises of pay or freedom. I fought alongside trained French soldiers and Indians and slaves who were as untrained as I.

When the war was over I returned home to find our land well-tended by Luke and by Phoebe but our circumstances very depleted and without the promised pay from the Continental Army I proceeded to apply for a bank loan and was turned down by every bank because I could not repay the bank in hard currency. Hard currency was scarce and the government refused to print more paper money. Instead the state of Massachusetts decided to tax heavily the poor farmers to fatten up their coffers which were in sad disrepair due to the war. If a farmer could not pay his taxes or get a loan to farm his land the state of Massachusetts took his land. If there was not enough land to satisfy his tax bill, the state of Massachusetts imprisoned the farmer leaving his family destitute.

Massachusetts Governor John Hancock was sympathetic to the farmers and refused to collect the unpaid taxes which were unfairly burdening so many poor farmers but he left his term early and his former opponent James Bowdoin who had run unsuccessfully for so many years against him took over. Bowdoin, a former merchant, was merciless in taking land and stock from farmers and jailing them to satisfy the debts of Europe merchants who were now demanding hard currency due to their own depletion after the war.

Job Shattuck, a professional soldier and large landowner in Groton who once fought for the British but joined the Continental Army when it was raised by General Washington took pity on the farmers' plight and led a large number of farmers to close the courts and stop prosecution of those who could not pay the unfair taxes. He was chased down by the Massachusetts militia for his troubles, wounded severely, jailed, sentenced to be hanged, and pardoned at the last minute by Governor Hancock.

I joined Daniel Shays, a poor farmhand before the war who because of his bravery was made a captain in the Continental Army but returned home to find debts mounted up in his absence and no way to collect pay promised him during the war.

We protested in Boston but were turned away there so we gathered a ragtag bunch of farmers to close the courts and break out the jailed farmers so they could take care of their families.

Our numbers swelled to four thousand with a lot of sympathizers but the state of Massachusetts raised a militia against us and beat us by might and by cunning. Most were later pardoned but a few of us with prices still on our heads escaped over the state line to Vermont and I went on to the wilderness of New York to escape hanging and seek my fortune whatever it turned out to be.

I came upon a place where a big lake the Indians called Ontario met with a river they called the Genesee. I figured it was a good spot to build a structure on with the abundance of water all around and plenty of farmland once it was cleared.

I set about to build a hut and sent for Josiah who was by now a strong sturdy lad and able to work alongside me to thatch a roof and clear some land. At night, to pass the time, I whittled him a crude instrument with holes for him to blow into and play a tune. We shared stories to catch up and he told me of all the doings of Ma and Pa and my brothers and sisters. I was heartened to hear that Pa had fashioned him a top when he was a younger lad because before I had left he had begged me for one but due to my absence I was unable to complete the task. I also learned that Pa had whittled a doll for both Mary and Patience and told them that I would have fashioned it myself had I been there so they could remember me.

The hut took shape rather quickly and I sent for Phoebe and the two girls. Phoebe brought with her some seeds to plant a garden and with my rifle I was able to provide a good deal of game for our larder. We never lacked for water with the beautiful blue waters of both the lake and river a few paces from our newly thatched hut. The land was fertile and with the fish Josiah brought in from our waters we thrived.

After a while settlers slowly joined us and we became a bustling settlement of sorts. What we lacked in armaments and numbers we made up in cunning and plainly much good sense. We turned the British from our shores twice when they attempted invasion during a war waged by our country to stop them from stealing the sailors from our newly formed navy and all they got were stores of grain which we surrendered gladly as we marched few around in circles to make them think we were many. We cleared the swamps when swamp fever threatened our small settlement.

During these years Josiah, Mary and Patience grew and Phoebe formed a small school to teach the children now arriving in our settlement. The government which had formed in Washington made our small settlement a U.S. port and I was appointed the first lighthouse keeper guiding ships to our shores and sending them off with goods to trade as far away as Europe. As the years passed lands were purchased near here by wealthy men from Massachusetts, New Jersey and the state of Maryland and named Rochesterville after Colonel Nathanial Rochester who purchased the most land which became a county seat and grew to a large trading center from a settlement of twelve to a settlement of seven hundred turning out nails and rope and woolens and milled grain and sending it by our great lake Ontario north and out to Europe with talk of bringing in the new railroad lines to send their goods out west.

I am happy for the growth here for it insures the future of Josiah and Mary and Patience. But, I long for the beautiful nights under the stars when we were first here and sat outside our newly-built hut in peace and silence except for the noisy chirping of the crickets who swarmed about us while we swapped stories or played a tune on our crudely fashioned instruments and the smaller children played tag and run or spun a top under the moonlight.

I miss my brothers and sisters but know that they have been safe and thriving as I am able to get a letter to them now and then and hear from them as they send one back. I wish only for their safety and comforts which I know they have. I have survived and thrived here only by the grace of Ma and Pa's early teachings and guidance and remember them in my prayers every night.

As I complete this record I wish only for the good fortune of my children and the success of this new country which we built out of a wilderness and has given us a home that gives us a reason to be thankful every day.

Respectfully Completed by Jeremiah Reed
Farmer, Soldier, and Lighthouse Keeper
in the Year 1820

I closed the journal and felt the silence of the house. Georgie was asleep and perhaps Mama as well. But, the energy of those who had gone before me and who I knew only through a pile of ragged and worn journals seemed still to fill the emptiness. I tugged on the string that hung from the bulb in the attic ceiling and shut off its light, leaving only the moonbeams making their way through the tiny attic window to light my way.

I crept softly down the winding attic stairway, Carrie's Dutch girl held tightly in my one hand, my other clutching the knotted and gnarled old pineywood railing. I headed for my room just as a heavy gust of wind blew in through the open windows, setting the lace curtains to fluttering wildly and my small lampshade hurtling to the floor. I slammed shut the windows and rescued the lampshade. A great clap of thunder sounded in the distance and lightening crackled in the darkened skies

above. I drifted off to sleep with the sound of heavy rains pelting the newly patched roof and visions of Mama's marshmallow cocoa steaming to warm the chill of an early autumn morning.

Chapter Eighteen

The Saturday morning Georgie and I set out to visit both Carrie and Will was a beautiful autumn morning. The leaves were turning their scarlet reds and golden yellows and the brightest orange hues that stood out from among the rest. The sun beat down upon us as we loaded up the truck with the jams and jellies that Mama insisted on sending and the oatmeal raisin cookies for Carrie and a special walnut cake for Will that Mama had just learned to make especially for him from an old recipe she found in the tattered family cookbook she kept in her special kitchen drawer.

I soaked up the warmth of the Indian summer day as I helped Georgie carefully place the two boxes that held the leather bags wrapped in a soft blue-green tissue paper that Georgie and I had tooled and sewn for Carrie and Will over many an evening and a Sunday afternoon. We hugged Mama goodbye and promised to call when we got to Carrie's school.

The back country roads were covered with the soft tar that the town and the county used to patch the potholes but Mama's old truck, despite its worn treads, managed to take us to the newly paved state highway which led to the Wells college campus. Georgie and I sang to pass the time and played guess the animal that put us into gales of laughter with the silly clues we both thought up. We stopped just once to revive ourselves with a box of animal crackers and a couple of sodas Mama never allowed in the house.

"Annie May, are we going to see where Carrie goes to school?"

"Of course, Georgie. Carrie's probably planning a tour for us already."

"Do you think when we get to Will's school he'll show me what he's learning about farming?"

"I think he can't wait to show you around the Ag campus. He wrote to Mama about how big the campus is and how many buildings they have devoted to agriculture. He wrote that there is so much for him to learn."

"Do you think I can learn about farming there too?"

"I think you can see everything they have if we have enough time. But, Uncle John says you're already a good farmer. He says you're a really good learner and lots of help when it comes to planting and harvesting."

"I can't wait till we pull in the cabbages, the feed corn, and the bush beans. Then, we can get to the haying. Uncle John says he's going to let me help with the baling this year."

"Well, that was always Will's job. And, Uncle John says you'll be a natural at that."

Georgie's head began to nod and a long-stifled yawn passed across his face as his head fell back against the pillow I had found to cushion him against the threadbare fake suede Mama had found as an end bolt to cover the seats with.

In the quiet that followed, as we drove through the towns of central New York, the signs in front of their schools asking us to slow though it wasn't a school day, the church spires rising above the storefronts and the auto shops, I began to muse about my own future. As we picked up speed on the open highway, the beautiful reds and rusts of the maples vying for my attention, the farmhouses, some set back and others perilously close to the road, with their hanging baskets of geraniums providing a flash of color as we went by, and their mums so neatly planted around their front stoops, I thought of what I might want to be. How I would spend my life.

Carrie had been certain she wanted to study art and Will had known he wanted to be a vet. But, I had kept my nose in books ever since I could remember. Studying English was far from practical as I had heard from the rumors flying about Sadie Mathews from town who a number of years ago as the first in her family to go to college chose to study English at a small college in the east and returned without a job to spend the next twenty years in sales at the local hardware store. Nevertheless, I couldn't think of anything else I wanted to do. I would find a way to talk to Mama about it.

As Wells loomed up before us I nudged Georgie gently as I wheeled the old truck onto the campus to find a proper parking place. Georgie yawned and looked around.

"Where will Carrie be?"

"She's at her dorm. It's called Leach. She gave us the name when she called Mama."

Students were everywhere, crisscrossing the campus in twos and threes, all anxious to find something or chatting away or just musing, a far-away look in their eyes.

It was easy to find Carrie's dorm. Georgie asked

everybody and they were all happy to point him in the right direction. As we neared the building, a structure once a very large house of beautiful brick, large long windows and a dormer attic, surrounded by a well-kept lawn and gardens, we spotted Carrie, her hand on her brow shading her eyes as she scoured the campus. Georgie broke into a run. Carrie caught him in a big hug as he landed on the portico.

"Gee, Squirrel," I gushed, stopped by the beauty of what was obviously the former home of a wealthy donor, "this place is beautiful."

"It is," said Carrie, "but it's not home." Her eyes for a moment were wistful, their deep, rich brown misted over despite her resolve, as she held Georgie tight, looking for sure like she'd never let him go.

"Do they have any frogs here?"

"I've found some peepers. They're hard to spot, but you can find them headed for the lake, sometimes in an evening."

As Georgie headed off to search for frogs along the expansive lawn, I sat with Carrie on one of the two lawn chairs available to students.

"Do you like it here, Carrie?" I asked, my voice

barely above a whisper, since it had been our custom since childhood never to pry.

"I like my art classes. I like the professors. They're very good at art and very patient. And, we only have about nine or ten in our classes.

"But, I miss riding that roan at the Taylor farm, even though his friskiness made me lose my way so many times, I miss spending hours in Mr. Peterson's store picking out just the right scarf, I miss Georgie pestering me to help him with his art project, and I miss Mama fussing over the hours we need to be back and telling us endlessly how to behave so we won't be seen as trash. And, you, Annie May, I miss our hours of gossip, especially in the moments we found to slip out to Strawberry Hill."

I knew that admission was tough for Carrie as we weren't a demonstrative family. I decided to make every moment of this visit count.

"Do you hear from Jamie, Carrie?"

"I do. He writes me almost every day. He's so faithful. But, that just makes me miss him more.

"He writes me about his classes and his professors. He's a good student, Annie May. He wants to succeed because he feels his parents have sacrificed to send him to school."

"Will you invite him for Thanksgiving or Christmas?"

"He has invited me for both or either. But, he understands how hard it is for me to spend the time with his family when I have always spent it with mine. I thought we might switch off for the holidays or invite his whole family to spend one of them with ours."

"Sounds like a good idea. Has he invited you for a Harvard weekend?"

"He has, but I know he isn't very social. He prefers to spend his time studying. He has big plans for himself after he graduates."

"Well, you can't spend your time mooning over him or you won't get your own work done."

"I know, Annie May. I don't know what to do."

"How about if I drive you to Boston for a weekend? You can spend time with Jamie and help him study and I can check out the latest big-city fashions and report to Mama."

"Gosh, Annie May, would you do that?"

"If Mama will part with the truck for a weekend."

"Thanks, Annie May. I can't wait to write to Jamie."

As Carrie mulled over the idea, Georgie returned with two peepers and a full sized frog, all wriggling to be let go. "Can we let them off at the lake, Carrie?"

"Of course, Georgie, I'm sure they'll like that. It would probably take them all day to get there."

As we all three went down to the shore of Lake Cayuga, its waters as blue as its reputation, we took in the beautiful brick buildings that held the classrooms, the beautiful old homes that housed the students, and the campus grounds covered by majestic evergreens and deciduous trees of all kinds, their leaves vying for brilliance in the autumn show. I was sure Carrie was shielded from the real world here.

Georgie let off his frogs as close to the water as he could get. We strolled back to the campus and lunch which Carrie had arranged.

Georgie was a celebrity in the campus dining hall and Carrie's friends fussed over him endlessly. We rushed as much as we could so we could squeeze in enough time to visit Will as well.

As we headed for the parking lot, Georgie burst out with news of the book bag, a fact he had wanted to keep as a surprise. Carrie drew him to her in a big bear hug. "Oh, Georgie, I can hardly wait to see it."

He presented the book bag with as much fanfare as he could muster in a parking lot. Carrie was moved to tears and gushed over the beautiful hand tooling, the neat seamless sewing, and the quality of the leather. She kept it on her lap as we headed for Cornell and Georgie fell asleep on her shoulder.

Carrie and I were silent on the half-hour trip to Cornell, partly to let Georgie sleep, partly because we were both lost in our own thoughts. College was a mixed bag for me. On the one hand, I was anxious to delve into studies that would keep me from the real world. On the other, the real world still had a strong hold on me.

"We're here," I announced, as we pulled into the city of Ithaca, its narrow sidewalks and kitschy cafes and shops home to the city's residents as well as the artsy students of Ithaca College and the swells of the thousands from Cornell. We drove up to the campus with difficulty, the steep hills working against the power of Mama's truck.

As we drove through college town, we took a deep breath. We had made it up the famous hills of Cornell. Georgie woke with a start.

"When can we see Will?"

"When we find the student union," I volunteered, keeping my eyes open for a parking space among the tightly packed cars that lined the streets at the edge of the enormous campus. "It's right next to the library. Will described it. We need to park the truck and start walking."

Georgie spotted a space in front of a large imposing building that had been set up on a hill above the roadway and we got out, immediately dwarfed by the large buildings above us. It was a long stretch to the student union with stops to ask directions of the many students who crowded the sidewalks, their desire to help interrupted only by gales of laughter and Saturday afternoon horseplay.

The student union was impressive, its gothic turn-of-the-century stone architecture a reminder of a more genteel era. Will was sitting in an armchair in the lobby, his nose in a book. Georgie ran straight for him, startling a student or two on the way.

"Hey, Georgie, I think you've grown a foot since I've seen you.

"Carrie, how's Wells?"

"Great. Keeping me busy."

"And, Annie May, it looks like you've added a few freckles."

I ignored Will's teasing and made plans for Carrie and me to meet Will back here after he and Georgie toured the Ag campus and saw all the ancient farm equipment and the modern inventions the school had such a hand in that Will had written Uncle John about.

Carrie and I spent the rest of the time in college town, Carrie with a cherry coke and me with my favorite malt that Danny Simpson, the soda fountain expert at Manning's Drugs, made so well. Students came and went, their lively chatter a backdrop to the little café we found between the hamburger stands and pizza shops.

"Gosh, Squirrel, I wouldn't be able to find my way around this campus. But it seems to suit Will's serious side. He has such a thirst for learning. Uncle John said he never saw a farmhand like Will."

"Will's special, Annie May. He's quiet. But, inside, it seems he's always thinking."

"Now, I can't decide what's better. A big college or a small one like Wells."

"You'll know when you start looking. The important thing is that they have the program you're looking for. For you, Annie May, they better have a library with lots and lots of books. I've never seen anyone read as much as you along with all the chores we had."

"Reading took me away. It took me to so many other worlds. I want to take those kids in town to those worlds. I want to show them there are other worlds besides the world of constant struggle."

"Well, other worlds can be exciting. But, the townies have had some good times, too. The excitement of the county fair. The sidewalks to skip rope on and play hopscotch. The old barns that hold old cars now to throw a ball against. And, everyone in the village to answer to because they care."

"Answering to old Mrs. Collins was always a chore. She was on her front porch in a rocker whenever I passed through town, sitting with her knitting and scouring the passers-by with those sharp eagle eyes and forever correcting my posture. And, never letting me pass until I told her what I was studying in school."

"She didn't favor bows or scarves and whenever she saw me she would lecture me on prim and proper dress.

"But, Annie May, I want to bring beautiful scarves and belts and buckles to the world. I want to make every town brighter."

"I know you will, Carrie. When you finish studying art, this world better watch out. I'm sure Mama will open one of her catalogs one day and find a line of scarves right in there you designed."

I picked up the check the waitress had dropped on our table some time ago. "We'd better get back. The sun will be going down and Georgie's probably asleep in one of those leather chairs in the student union."

As we walked back to the building the students called The Straight the sun began to set behind us. Its golden brilliance was majestic above the mauves and pinks, yellows and oranges that muted the twilit sky. The autumn leaves were all around us, crunching beneath our feet, and the haze of the nearby town so near beneath us.

Will gave us a proper sendoff at the truck and promised Georgie he would keep the book bag which he deemed a real work of art forever. Georgie switched from chattering endlessly to falling asleep on Carrie's shoulder. Carrie hugged Georgie and me as tight as I can remember as we left her at her dorm and as we headed home Georgie began counting the stars, dozing off when the numbers began to exceed his grasp. As we pulled into the old, familiar driveway rutted out all the way to the barn, scattering barn cats everywhere, Mama's anxious silhouette was visible through the dimly lit kitchen windows, left open to the raw brisk chill of the autumn evening. I raced Georgie to the door, both of us giggling as we dropped on the faded yellow linoleum. I rose and headed for my room, snuggling under the beautiful white quilt with the hearts and roses that had kept me warm since childhood. My college plans would have to wait till morning.

Chapter Nineteen

The chill of the winter had worn off and the spring of 1955 was filled with sunshine and meadow daisies and the deep vibrant purple of the lilac blossoms behind the barn, their blooms ever faithful in the month of May.

Georgie rose every morning to check the seed catalogs. He had been promoted from gofer and lackey with his own acre filled with the vegetables he chose to full partner over the whole farm, at least in choice of crops. He had been a good predictor with his own acreage and probably the most popular as the youngest in sales at both the Rochester and Syracuse markets the two previous seasons.

The corn was already in and the soybeans were ready for planting. It was wheat and cabbage next and Georgie was mulling over the varieties. The Taylors regularly outgrew Uncle John in wheat and Georgie wanted to find a cabbage that would outshine the output of Phelps which was pretty well known as the cabbage capital of the state.

"Hey, Georgie," I said, as he ambled into my room on a lazy Sunday afternoon while Mama sewed a new skirt for Carrie and I tried to catch up on my homework after a long and busy day the day before selling the new spring line at Peterson's dry goods to almost everybody in town. "How's the cabbage search?"

"Gosh, Annie May, I think I found a way to beat out Phelps. We can start a crop of early cabbage which almost no one else grows around here and we can beat them to market because they grow theirs to harvest late in time for the cabbage festival in fall."

"Great idea, Georgie. I bet Uncle John will be so proud of you for thinking it out."

"Well, I know he'll like this cabbage. According to the catalogue it's easy to grow, low maintenance, and a really great yield."

"It sounds like this is a good answer to the Phelps problem."

"I can hardly wait to tell Uncle John. I've been searching for weeks."

"Did you get the old tractor all greased up and running?"

173

"Aw, yeah, Annie May, we did that weeks ago. Uncle John says I have a real knack for mechanics."

"Maybe you would like to be a mechanic when you finish school like Jasper Thomas. He can fix anything."

"I don't want to fix things, Annie May. I want to grow things. You should see all the things they're growing at Will's school. They're growing cabbages bigger than I've ever seen even in the catalogues. And, the peppers and tomatoes get nearly 60 to a plant."

"Papa always said you were a born farmer, Georgie. I guess he was right."

"I can't wait to ride the tractor at planting time. The air's so fresh, the sun's just waiting to warm the seedlings, and the rains come down if you're lucky to make them sprout. And, no one's out there but the barn cats.

"Of course fighting the insects is hard, but Uncle John has some good secrets for that. And, the wet and dry seasons. But, last year we had a good harvest and I sold everything in my acre."

At that Mama entered the room, her arms full of the new skirt she just finished for Carrie. "Are you still talking farming, Georgie? Your Papa always counted on you to help him run this farm when you got older.

When you were no bigger than a cub he had plans on how he was going to talk old Taylor into parting with some of his acres and make a really big spread here. "Tyler Parker and Son" he was going to call it. Your Papa was a real dreamer…"

Mama's voice trailed off as it always did when she talked about Papa. I decided to pick up the slack. "Georgie, if you finish your homework, I'll race you to the barn and we can see if Calico had her kittens yet. And, we can peek at the robin's nest and see if the eggs are hatched. And, if we make it to Strawberry Hill and the berries are ripe whoever picks the most gets to help Mama with a pie."

"Now, Annie May, I don't know if I'll have time to bake a pie today."

But, I knew Mama would do anything to please Georgie, especially since Carrie was gone and she tried to fill the gap. Georgie picked up his pace and set out for his room.

"Annie May, have you heard from any colleges?"

"Not yet, Mama, but I'm hoping for Syracuse. That way I can save money by living at home."

"Syracuse is a big school. Most of the students are from big cities. Are you sure you can handle it?"

"I think so. They have writers from all over the world teaching there. I would get to study with some of the best."

"Well, I hope you get in. But, you can't put all your eggs in one basket."

I know Mama was trying to keep me from disappointment since Carrie always got what she wanted being the pretty and popular one. But, I was determined not to give up.

"I'll try to remember that, Mama." Nevertheless, I crossed my fingers behind my back hoping for some luck in the matter.

Mama hung Carrie's skirt in her closet. "Annie May, how about a taffy pull after supper? I think Georgie could use one. He's kind of down on his grades."

"I think that would be fun, Mama," I said, mentally figuring how I would finish the mountain of homework I had to postpone because of work. But, I didn't want to disappoint Georgie. I knew how he missed Carrie and Will.

"I've got peppermint and chocolate and I might have some strawberry."

"All of Carrie's and Will's favorites."

"Well, Will's been keeping up with the latest in

farming with Georgie. And, I know it has helped Uncle John as well.

"And, I know how homesick Carrie must be even though she hardly lets on."

"Okay, I'll package it up and send it out tomorrow. And, we might as well make some biscuits for Jester. Georgie never asks but I know he has a special pact with Will to keep Jester in dog treats."

As Mama's steps retreated down the creaky treads of the old back stairway, making its way to the entrance of the kitchen, the large soup pot perennially on the back burner, Mama's favorite pots hanging over the extra-large white stove, I thought of the future.

Carrie, who was as passionate as she was impractical, needed a settling influence. Mama had been lost without Papa and his dreams. Georgie was headed for farming. As for me, I knew I wanted to teach but I felt a restlessness I couldn't identify. A restlessness born of years of responsibility taken for granted.

But, I couldn't abandon Mama. I decided to ponder it all another time and give my attention to the pile of unfinished homework still sitting on my desk.

I looked out the window toward the sun-drenched fields for inspiration, the rich dark loamy soil already tilled and plowed, awaiting spring planting. A robin perched on the old red maple out back and a blue jay chased away a cardinal from the new bird feeder Uncle John had just put up beside the barn. I decided to move along as swiftly as I could so we could make it to Strawberry Hill before the sun sank below the soft azure blues of the nearly cloudless sky.

Chapter Twenty

The blue jays and the cardinals chattered overhead as Carrie and I pulled out of the Wells College parking lot to head for Boston. Jamie had invited Carrie for Harvard's annual spring weekend and I would be a guest of a friend of his he had set up as an escort for the occasion. Carrie was overjoyed to be seeing Jamie again but my knees were turning weak at the thought of providing a fourth in what would ordinarily have been a threesome.

I had never dated a college boy much less a lot of my high school classmates and the thought produced a fear I had never experienced before. But, for Carrie's sake I was determined to reach down for a courage I had reserved for riding bareback on a newly broken horse or jumping into the icy cold pond in winter on a dare.

Carrie had brought some egg salad sandwiches, two bottles of iced tea, and a variety of strawberry, raspberry, and fig-filled pastry rolls she had talked the dining room pastry chef into parting with. She was hunkered down for the fairly long trip to Boston.

"Gosh, Annie May, I wonder what Jamie has planned for us?"

"Whatever it is I hope it involves a place to stay."

"He has made arrangements for us to stay at Radcliffe with a couple of his roommates' dates."

"Sounds good. I packed a couple of sleeping bags in case.

"Carrie, do you have a dress for the dance?"

"I made my dress. I couldn't wait to design it. Laurie Sue Malloy who lives next to me lent me her sewing machine. It's the latest, with a buttonholer and seam stitcher attached.

"It's the most beautiful green silk, with velvet accents, and a large velvet bow in the back. I can't wait to wear it."

"I'm sure Jamie will think you're the most beautiful girl there."

"I don't know, Annie May. I suppose those Radcliffe girls are knockouts. Not country girls like us."

"I think your dress and a French twist with those tortoise shell combs from Aunt Maybelle that I know you prize will make you a standout no matter how many city girls attend."

"I hope so. And, what did you bring to wear to the dance?"

"Hank Peterson let me choose from the new stock that just came in. I got my first pick of the prom dresses. I didn't have a chance to get it fitted, but it will just have to do."

"No problem. I brought my sewing basket with us for last minute alterations. We'll make it fit."

Just like Carrie to think of everything when it comes to style and fashion. Although I wasn't looking forward to being the belle of the ball at least I wouldn't stand out if it was up to Carrie. However, I wasn't certain how she was going to make a light blue taffeta conform to my fairly athletic form. But, I knew I would have to develop some patience while I stood on a rise and Carrie worked her magic. After all, this was her important weekend and I knew I couldn't let her down.

The light drizzle that had been pelting the truck for the last half hour let up and the sun came out, bringing Carrie out of her funk and into her bright side. "Jamie has asked one of his roommates to make us a foursome. His name is Maxwell Oliver. He says Max is very shy and has hardly asked any girls out. But, he says that you are just the one to bring him out and get him to be more social. Harvard has a lot of activities and Jamie thinks Max is missing a lot of college life."

"I'll do my best. But, all I've done with boys is arm wrestle, chase loose horses and race bareback, and go swimming in the ponds out back beyond the meadows. None of them have ever asked me to a dance.

"If it wasn't for Miss Lewis in gym this year who insisted everyone learn the fox trot and that new swing dancing that's just coming in in case we got asked to the prom I wouldn't know a step. But, I think I still have two left feet."

"Girls just have to follow. The boy is supposed to lead. So, you just depend on your partner. It should be easy."

Carrie, worn from pulling all-nighters on her art projects, fell asleep as soon as we left the first rest stop. It was left to me to watch the road and contemplate my future, at least my immediate future. I fell to imagining what Maxwell Oliver might be like. At first I had him big and athletic and looking good in a tux. Next, slight and small with a bad complexion. I decided to wait and see and turned to counting how many houses needed paint in the small towns we encountered as we left the turnpike.

Carrie awoke as we pulled into Boston. Despite our carefully mapped out route we were left to asking directions of almost every gas station attendant on the way to Cambridge. Nevertheless, we arrived at almost the appointed hour. Jamie was waiting as planned. I left Carrie and Jamie to a private reunion while I fiddled with the luggage in the back but Jamie pulled me out of the truck to welcome me as well.

"Welcome, Annie May. I have great accommodations for you both in the Radcliffe dorms. Two girls away for the weekend but they're very willing to lend you their room."

"Thanks so much, Jamie," I said, with as much enthusiasm as I could muster after the long drive. "I know we can use it. If you show us how to get there, I can unpack for both of us and maybe take a nap while you show Carrie the campus."

"I'd like to show you the campus as well, Annie May. And, I know my friend Max is anxious to meet you. So, why don't I ride with you to Radcliffe, get you settled , and pick you both up after you get some rest and freshen up. I know it's been a long drive.

"Thanks, Jamie. Sounds good."

Although Jamie and Carrie only had eyes for each other on the way to Radcliffe, Jamie's manners kept him from ignoring me completely. We shared some small talk while Carrie remained uncharacteristically quiet and I pulled from my body of knowledge to sound as intelligent as I could.

Radcliffe, the women's college across the Cambridge Common from Harvard, was as stately and classically built but not as imposing. Women crossed the campus in easy chatter, dressed in classic sweaters and plaid skirts. Its quiet gentility was far from the rough and forthright world both Carrie and I knew, but I was determined to fit in for Carrie's sake, at least for the weekend.

Jamie took our suitcases and led us toward a beautiful brick building on what he called the quad. "This is Eliot. I can only go as far as the entrance hall. But, I'll be back to pick you up as soon as you get settled. If you need anything, just use one of the hall phones to call my dorm room."

At that, Jamie pressed the empty dorm room key into Carrie's hand and we were on our own. Carrie was as quiet as any mouse as we headed up the stairs, all the newels of the carefully polished rails beautifully carved and hand turned. Quiet reigned as we looked for the number and found it down a very long corridor recently painted in a very soft pastel shade of muted green.

We opened the door to a dark paneled room with pennants and memorabilia hung on thumbtacks, pegs and nails in every empty space. The beds were covered in beautiful quilted spreads of deep green. Shoes were everywhere.

We quickly found the showers, choosing our most casual outfits to slip into. As Carrie called Jamie, I crossed my fingers behind my back. I was going to need all the luck I could get to fit into a Harvard College weekend.

Chapter Twenty-One

Harvard Yard was surrounded by the most stately buildings I had ever seen. Dormitories, libraries and classrooms lined the perimeters of the grassy flatlands of the famous Yard, backed by some of the oldest college buildings in the nation. Students, oblivious to its awe-inspiring history, strolled the Yard, yawning after a late Friday night fraternity event, or loudly and excitedly making plans for the evening's big dance.

Jamie, excited to give us a tour of the campus he obviously loved, pointed out to us the many architectural details hearkening back to the eighteenth century and a detailed history of almost each and every building we passed.

Jamie had made plans to meet Max at one of the libraries where he obviously spent much of his time. As we neared the moment my knees went weak despite my intent to act as casual as I could.

Maxwell Oliver was nothing like I had imagined him. Neither acned or big and beautifully built he was pretty average. Medium height, glasses with frames that fit his face, and clothes so carefully pressed and tailored they would never have found their way into any of Mama's catalogues. His shyness was obvious, as he looked down at his feet instead of at us, but so was his generosity.

We found Max at the appointed place in the beautiful brick building that housed the library. He immediately stood as he saw us enter and shoved a box of dried fruit into Jamie's outstretched hand.

"Would anyone like a dried apricot?" he mumbled, as he looked down at the beautifully polished floor.

"Maybe we better do the introductions first," Jamie laughed, as he brought me forward to introduce me.

"Max, this is your date for the dance tonight. May I present Miss Annie May Parker from New York. "

"How do you do?" said Max, his face turning red but lifting his gaze to meet mine.

"How do you do," I returned, my knees weakening only slightly.

"And this," Jamie continued, "is Carrie Parker, her sister and my date for the weekend."

"It is nice to meet you, Miss Parker."

Carrie took Max's hand and shook it. "It's nice to

meet you too Max. I hope we didn't disturb your studying."

As an answer Max invited us to join him for a snack and a stroll around Harvard Square, a short walk from the Yard and an obvious student hangout from the rigors of studying. "My treat," he stated, still studying the floor as he spoke.

Although Max was shy, he was forceful in leading the way to the Square, as he explained most students called it. Jamie and Carrie hung back a bit, so it was left to me to follow Max's strident lead, and I was up to it, gaining a second wind as the afternoon wound down.

"You'll like the Square," Max said, to no one in particular.

I ventured an "I'm sure we will," but Max kept heading for the Square with an intent I'm sure he reserved for every activity he indulged himself in.

As we left the Yard and the Square opened up I stopped. This was shopper's heaven for a small town girl like me. The department stores loomed big but the five and dime stores looked even better. Casual restaurants were everywhere and book stores lined every street. A co-op which doubled for a general store held everything anyone would ever want. And, it was all overseen by a policeman in a very high turret in the center of the Square.

Students strolled the streets, many with ice cream cones in hand, all in casual dress, chatting wildly and heading for their favorite haunts. "How about the Tasty?" Max shouted to Jamie. Jamie nodded in agreement but kept his attention on Carrie.

The Tasty Sandwich Shop, or the Tasty, as it had been known to Harvard students for decades, was a small one-room diner in the center of Harvard Square. Its narrow lunch counter covered in old yellow linoleum was crammed with locals, visitors, Harvard students and professors, blue and white collar workers, and just about anybody who came in from off the street. The quarters were small but the conversation was lively. The cooks chatted with the customers while turning hotdogs and hamburgers on the open grill, filling orders at the most rapid pace I had ever seen. A large map covered the back wall with pins for every locale the diner had received postcards from, most from former customers, many of them now famous, but all reliving their days at the Tasty.

Max stood behind a couple who seemed to be finishing up so Carrie and I could get a stool. As they left, Max swooped down to grab both seats, despite his shyness an expert in diner strategy.

Jamie and Max stood behind us and ordered. Jamie, anxious to include me, shouted over the snippets of the loudest conversations I had ever heard, "So what do you think of Harvard, Annie May?"

"It's sure different than Mayberry and Baldwinsville Central."

Jamie laughed. "It was hard for me to adjust to and I come from Manhattan. New Yorkers should be able to handle anything. But, college life at Harvard was new to me. I intend to make everything I can out of it.

"The professors will help you all they can if you have an interest in your studies. And, I have made many friends here. We have formed the best study groups on campus."

It was plain to see that Jamie was here to succeed. It was less obvious what Max was here for. I decided to leave him alone in his own little world. Although he was mostly speechless, I could see that he was taking everything in in his own quiet way."

Jamie handed us our hotdogs spread thick with mustard but the elbow room at the counter was pretty limited. Carrie and I nibbled genteelly as best we could but we lost the battle to keep the mustard on the hotdog. I knew my light green shirt had seen better days but I also knew with Carrie's knowledge of spotting laundry and bleach it would be fresh by morning.

"We better get the girls back to the dorm, Max, so they can get ready for the dance tonight. We've deprived them of their beauty rest long enough."

As we walked back to the Radcliffe campus, the sunset beautiful over Harvard Square, I thought of the many sunsets I had watched from Strawberry Hill. I vowed to stand as still as I could without complaint when Carrie took in my dress for the dance tonight. As we strolled alongside manicured lawns and carefully tended gardens, full of the most cultivated blossoms I had ever seen, I glanced at Carrie, her face aglow in the rising moonlight, her arm slipped through Jamie's, and I knew that for her, this would have to be a perfect weekend.

Chapter Twenty-Two

The floors were polished and red, white and blue lights hung from everywhere for the annual spring weekend dance at Harvard. Black and white dinner jackets mingled with all manner of gowns as the famous Lester Lanin society band, recruited many years in advance, set up to play the evening away with pop tunes of the day and Broadway numbers I had never heard.

Jamie was anxious to show Carrie a good time. He had brought her a beautiful orchid wrist corsage which his mother had sent, a newly developed orchid recently named and bred by a member of her highly specialized orchid society. Carrie was thrilled, especially because it blended so well with the green silk she had spent so long designing and perfecting.

As for me, Max had also brought me an orchid as well from the local florist. I had never had an orchid before so I felt quite grand as he pinned the corsage to the light blue taffeta Carrie had tamed to fit my modest but rather athletic frame. I had added a pair of rhinestone earrings and a matching clip to my hair that

Carrie had lent me in a bid to blend in to the sophistication I saw all around me.

The Harvard seal was represented everywhere, on a crimson banner hung on a wall behind the tuxedoed band members, and on the small round tables set off to the side covered with the most pristine and carefully pressed white linen I had ever seen.

Radcliffe dates outnumbered the out-of-towners and all were dressed in the latest and most costly fashions. But, to me, Carrie outshone them all.

"Would you like to dance, Annie May?"

"Of course," I said, mentally hoping Miss Lewis' admonitions and Max's skill would keep me upright on the floor which now looked like the face of Mama's prized bureau silver looking glass.

To my surprise, Max whirled me around the dance floor with perfect ease, his hand hard-pressed against my back to keep me steady, even dipping in the final phase of the tune without a mishap.

To my relief, he suggested we sit the next one out. "You dance beautifully, Annie May. You have such a good sense of rhythm."

I was proud as a peacock but I made sure not to show it. No boy had ever praised me except in arm wrestling and horse roping. "Would you like something to drink?"

"A soda would be fine," I answered weakly.

"Great. We have a fine brand of soda water highly prized by the bartenders who think of themselves as mixologists. I'll be back in a jiffy."

While Max was gone, I used the time to survey the crowd. Diamonds were the norm as accessories for the beautiful ball gowns and cultured pearls that looked like they had been in the family for generations. Would Carrie be happy in a crowd like this?

I looked at Carrie dancing away the evening with Jamie and decided to dismiss my thoughts for the moment.

Max returned with a plate of fruit, a stemmed crystal with soda water half-poured, and a glass of scotch he deemed the best on the planet. "The bartender, who is a fraternity brother of a friend of mine, had the best fruit brought in from the kitchen to add to your soda water. I hope you don't mind that I took the liberty."

Max was a strange bird alright, asking my permission to treat me like I was European royalty. I added a beautifully cut lemon, a strawberry, and a wedge of lime. The flavor was divine and I decided to savor the moment.

"Annie May, would you like to take a walk around the grounds? I can show you the place that is my most favorite when I want to get away from it all."

"I'd be glad to Max. I think a walk in the fresh spring air would be just the thing to revive me."

The Yard was literally deserted as we strolled its grassy grounds save for some lights burning in corners of the almost empty buildings. Max walked slowly, the scent of spring air all about us, the gardens lit by tiny little lights that gave them an eerie glow, and the sky above us dark and still, a new moon in the midst of crowds of stars.

As we neared a very small path, now lit only by moonlight, Max took a sharp right, motioning me to follow. We walked through bowers and bowers of trees until we came to a small clearing. "This is where I spend most of my time when I don't have my nose glued to a book in the dorms or in the library."

I surveyed the clearing. Grass a little less manicured than the rest of the campus, gardens sporting the blooms of spring, a bulb garden with the vibrant hues of carefully chosen tulips, the golden yellow of daffodils, and grape hyacinths lining its borders. And, all surrounded by stately oaks, maples, hickories, and elms. A flowering mountain ash stood in the corner and an ancient weeping willow hugged the far end.

Max beckoned me toward a wrought iron bench set in the middle of the clearing. The small plate fastened so securely to the back announced the donors as the class of 1918. Max motioned me to sit.

We sat, both of us in wordless wonder contemplating the stars. Max broke the silence. "I have found peace here, Annie May. In this little spot. More than I have ever known."

"It is beautiful," I said.

"I am an only child of parents who have succeeded in what they set out to do but had very little time for me. It's not that they meant to neglect me, it's just that they were very driven.

"I was shifted from one relative to another while they made a name in Europe or elsewhere. I was raised by nannies and sent to boarding school at an early age.

"My classmates made fun of me because I had bad skin, had a stutter, and was very shy. My skin cleared thanks to a caring doctor and my stutter disappeared after a lot of hard work on my own, working in secret with exercises I found in books. But, the memory of the taunts stayed with me.

"I came to Harvard because my father was a Harvard grad and my mother a Radcliffe alum."

"Do you like it here?"

"I like it as well as any other place. But, I feel lost. I didn't rush a fraternity because I thought I wouldn't get in. And, the independents seem to keep to themselves."

"Maybe they're just scared like you are. Maybe if you made the first move they'd join you in some cause or study group."

"I never thought of it like that. I just keep thinking they're sneering at me underneath like the boys in boarding school."

" Jamie seems to think a lot of you."

"Jamie is different, Annie May. He's friendly and outgoing. He's good through and through. We hit it off from the start."

Max looked at his watch and rose. "I guess I've bored you long enough. We should get back to the dance before they think we've left for good."

"I haven't been bored, Max. You're an interesting

person. I know you're going to go somewhere someday."

"Thanks for the faith. Most girls are turned off by serious talk."

Our walk back to the dance was filled with detours. Max was anxious to show me every building he had frequented since he'd been at Harvard. He was especially fond of the government building. And, history seemed to fascinate him.

"I was thinking of a double major in history and government. But, my family for generations have been business moguls. And, I don't think I have the personality or stamina for politics."

"I think you can be whatever you want. Back home we set the bar pretty high. I have beaten boys at horseshoes who have been champions and outrun a number of them."

"Well, I'll keep it in mind. But, I don't want to disappoint my family."

When we arrived back at the dance the crowd had thinned out and the band was getting ready for their final number. Carrie and Jamie were still dancing even though the music had stopped.

Max led me to the dance floor. "Let's take one last spin," he said, as he whirled me around in a perfect fox trot to the strains of "Good Night Ladies."

We walked back to Eliot, the balm of the spring air gently wafting about us, Jamie with his arm securely around Carrie. The new moon, so visible in the clear sky, signaled to me a beginning. Perhaps I had gotten into Syracuse.

As we entered the Eliot dorm room I kicked off my shoes. The residents of the room were mysterious only by their absence. Their presence was everywhere.

I carefully moved several bottles of expensive perfume to lay my small belongings on the carefully appointed cherry dresser, cherubs carved into its two upper drawers and a cherry-framed mirror set atop it. I said a hasty goodnight to Carrie.

As I turned down the bedspread and opened the shades to see the stars, the weariness of the day settled in. I decided to count rest stops instead of sheep and map out the journey back home. I knew it would be a difficult goodbye for Carrie.

Chapter Twenty-Three

Summer brought both Carrie and Will back home, Carrie to Sandler's Drugs in town to make sodas and hot fudge sundaes for the teenagers who gathered there in the heat of a late afternoon or evening and Will back to farming. Georgie was excited to show Will the fort he had made in a tree with the help of Uncle John and the art project he had done by himself waiting for Carrie's approval.

As for me, I was busy planning out my freshman year at Syracuse where I had finally been accepted. It was worth the wait. The course work looked exciting and I could see there was so much I could learn about books and the great authors who had written them.

The meadows were filled with wild flowers and the deep yellow of the black-eyed Susans and the pure white of the summer daisies wound their way through the tall grasses of the meadows along with the soft, pale yellow of the buttercup and the muted lavender of phlox.

Georgie was by Will's side the minute he got back home, talking farming, jumping into as many ponds as they had time for, and throwing sticks and balls for Jester to fetch. Uncle John had hired Will back, anxious to learn the latest in the techniques of sowing, the cross-breeding that was on the cutting edge, and the exciting advancements in farm machinery.

My graduation party had come and gone, attended by a multitude of relatives from as far away as Texas, anxious to soak up the lush valleys and hills of central New York, its many lakes, and its endless views of geological wonders. Cousins I barely knew stayed on to help with the dishes, camp out under the trees behind the corn and soy bean fields, and learn to ride bareback over at the Taylor farm.

Will had gotten me a journal for graduation and I was anxious to fill it. Mama was happy to have a full house again and I decided to make my way to the attic to escape her notice. As I crouched in the corner with the two small windows opened hoping to let the heat out, I wondered what our ancestors, so neatly tied up in the journals under the wedding dress, would think of us. Would they find us soft? Perhaps more spoiled than they with our modern conveniences, indoor plumbing, and a barn full of machinery to farm with?

I decided to open the last of the five journals. Its cover was nearly off the binding and its inside pages fragile. I carefully untied the ribbon holding it together and gently blew the dust off.

A note was written in Granny's hand.

My Dear Children,

I am setting down the tale of a woman named Mirabela who was your great-great grandmother of whom I am a direct descendant.

Mirabela was born into a band of roving gypsies who roamed as outcasts from land to land in Europe. She was known as Bela by all who knew her because the gaiety of her laughter matched the sound of the church bells that called the townspeople to morning worship.

The gypsies survived by luring the townspeople to their camps with the promise of fortune telling and the beautiful gypsy music that enchanted them around an open fire. Bela learned the art of palm reading and how to uncover the mysteries of the crystal ball by helping the women set up the tables and collecting the gold coins the townspeople left behind.

Though Bela liked the freedom of the wandering gypsy band, she often yearned for a settled life like the townsfolk she saw who came to the camps for a night of music and dancing but returned to their homes where there was a chance for honest trade and schools for their children.

Bela kept her longings to herself since she admired both her mother, who was beautiful and raven-haired with ringlets that reached far below her shoulders, and her father, who was the leader of their gypsy band. At night she would watch her father fiddle and her mother dance, her jewelry and bangles gleaming in the moonlight, her brightly colored skirt forming the most beautiful patterns along with her lively step.

As the gypsies wandered, Bela heard tales of a land across the sea that had streets paved with gold and where all were welcome. When she reached eighteen years old, Bela left for America.

The entire gypsy band saw her off. They presented her with enough gold coins to pay for her passage in steerage on an ocean liner that was creaky but still seaworthy. Her mother gave her a crystal ball and her father a beautiful fiddle. The rest, her friends since birth, gave her many colorful scarves, a stew of onions, hot peppers, and slivers of beef and game, and some gold coins to help her make her way in what they saw as a mystical New World.

When Bela arrived in America, she found the streets paved with cobblestone and brick, not gold, and gypsies unwelcome. She did her best to hide her identity and pursued her quest to settle down.

She traveled west, working at menial labor, far from the cities that had shunned her. As she went, admiring the beauty of this new land, she came upon a settlement of only a few dozen people that neither welcomed her or shunned her.

There she settled, happy to have a place of her own. She took two small rooms over the general store in exchange for scrubbing the floors and watching the store at night when the owners went home to their small farmhouse a short distance away.

The town had no name and its main street held

only the general store and a hitching post. Survival was hard-scrabble, pulling a few straggly crops from land that was barely arable, with hens and chickens and, if lucky, a goat or two.

Bela set up shop, pulling her crystal ball from the burlap sack she had so lovingly kept it in. At first no one came, but soon curiosity overtook their reluctance, and Bela was paid in chicken eggs and goat's milk.

As the two traders in the town became her best customers, listening to her tales of the future almost nightly, word spread to the towns and cities they traveled to, bringing eventual crowds to the settlement that had no name.

Although the visitors were a motley bunch, some dressed in leather breeches and some in gingham with bonnets of straw and silk, others in plain homespun, they all brought some form of wisdom to the settlement that had so far known only hard-scrabble living.

They brought with them the knowledge of how to fertilize the barely arable land, and how to irrigate it when the summer sun threatened to scorch the crops they had so carefully sown in the spring.

As the number of visitors grew, the settlers decided to give their town a name. They called it Hope.

Bela continued to scrub the floors of the general store and as she did so she noticed a farmer of modest stature with sandy brown hair and eyes as blue as the azure stone she had seen her gypsy band gather in their travels. Despite her shyness, she asked him to dine with her in her two small rooms.

He introduced himself as Simon Westerveld but gave her no more information than that. She soon took a shine to him and he to her.

They spent their time eating the stews Bela cooked that she remembered from her childhood. He was enchanted by the peals of her sunny laughter that echoed the church bells she had left behind and she was grateful for the strength of his serious, caring nature and the twinkle that seemed to never leave his eyes.

They were married shortly after and moved

into the simple log cabin he had erected when he had come to the settlement of Hope.

Simon worked hard to provide for Bela and she for him. She took her fortune telling to the camps of the visitors that streamed in to hear her tales of the future. She played her fiddle for them in the moonlight and taught them the gypsy dances.

Soon there was gaiety in the settlement that had so far had none. Travelers came from all over to take part in the yearly fair the settlers set up to celebrate their harvest. Bela took in many gold coins with her fortune telling and fiddled the night away, dancing under the moon with skirts of the brightest colors and scarves about her long black ringlets that fell far below her shoulders.

Bela's fortune telling brought many visitors to Hope and prosperity to the town. A hotel was raised next to the general store and a number of small shops along with it, including a blacksmith shop, a hardware store, and a small shop filled with the artisan works of the locals.

As the town of Hope prospered, so did Simon's farm. As the years went by, there were many mouths to feed for Bela and Simon were blessed with many children, all who worked the farm as they grew. Simon was filled with pride as he raised a sign with large, black letters over the barn he had built behind the simple log farmhouse that read "Westerveld & Sons."

Bela and Simon lived a long and happy life. As Bela lay on her deathbed, she confessed to Simon that she had never been able to predict the future nor had she ever been able to see anything as she gazed into her crystal ball. But, she had seen the hope in the eyes of the visitors who had traveled to their town for her predictions and had not wanted to disappoint them.

Simon laid Bela to rest in the small family plot on a hillside beyond the fields and next to a meadow that brought many wildflowers in early spring alongside their two little ones they had lost to the scourge of scarlet fever.

Visitors streamed in to the gravesite which Simon faithfully tended to hear what they were certain was the voice of Bela's spirit with predictions for the future. They left flowers and gold coins of gratitude which Simon gave to the schoolmaster for chalk and books for the schoolhouse which the townsfolk had built for the children of Hope.

Here Granny added a note.

For many years your Papa journeyed to the town of Hope to hear Bela's spirit predict the future. He was certain that the omens she foresaw were responsible for our good fortune in the generous bounty we almost always reaped at harvest.

I closed the journal gently, careful not to disrupt its fragile pages, bound it with its ribbon, and laid it back in its place beneath the other volumes. I crept down the stairs and slipped out the kitchen door, the aroma of roast chicken following me as I went. Mama was preparing a send-off supper for the cousins who were leaving tomorrow at sunrise.

I kicked off my shoes and ran to the barn to pull off the pail from the rusty nail that had held it since my early childhood. I would go to Strawberry Hill and harvest the last of the berries. I ran through the tall grasses of the meadow now rife with wildflowers and a soft, summer rain that brought a gentle mist and fog to the horizon.

As I walked back under a muted sunset of mauves and pinks sharing a slightly overcast sky, I was lost in thought of my own as yet unfulfilled future. I picked up my pace as I went. Mama would need help in the kitchen.

Chapter Twenty-Four

The first day of classes at Syracuse University was a balmy Indian summer day, almost tropical. Buildings of stone with formal columns and rooftop turrets stood side by side with buildings that followed the simpler lines of modern architecture. Stately evergreens, sycamores and shady maples dotted the grassy quad, dwarfing the students who filled the crisscrossing sidewalks in a hurry to find a classroom before the bell tower chimes rang out the hour.

A gentle wind ruffled my hair and blew about the leaves of the trees as I searched for the Hall of Languages and the freshman English class I had been assigned. As I came upon it, three rooftop turrets adding elegance to a weathered limestone façade, I climbed the steps and followed the stream of students pushing their way through a large front door, oblivious of the imposing pillars and the ancient-styled arch above it.

I found my classroom, the last at the end of a long, dimly-lit hallway, and settled on a second row seat. The boy behind me, tall and lanky, with a head of tousled brown hair gleaming in the morning sunlight streaming in through the long, large open windows, scoured the room and settled in beside me, juggling an armful of books and an open bag of peanuts.

"Care for a peanut?"

"No thanks."

"I'm Jeb Westfield. From Brooklyn. Originally from Westchester County but my dad lost his business to a corporate giant.

"I suppose you think me forward, and maybe I am, but you looked friendly and I'm not about to get knocked under by a super sophisticate from Manhattan or Long Island. This place scares me."

"Me too."

"Good. Maybe we can form an alliance of two and keep down the pseudo stuff."

"I'm not so sure."

"We can talk about it over a coke after class."

Before I could answer, the instructor put aside his papers and rose, waiting for the last straggler to come through the open door. As the seats filled, he closed the door and stood beneath the blackboard at the head of the class, his casual dress, black pants, black shirt, and black tied boots, a departure from the suits I had seen so far in administration.

"Hi. I'm Richard Anders. I'm a last year grad student and I will be your instructor for English 107 which is introductory English required for all freshmen.

"You will all be going on to major in a variety of disciplines. Our goal is to insure that you will be able to communicate with your colleagues and the public, if it is necessary, in clear and concise English.

"We will be covering the basic rules of composition and will brush up on grammar and language usage.

"Freshman English is a course generally hated by all incoming freshman. Please give it a try, and please have fun with it.

"There will be no assignment today to give you a chance to become oriented on the campus. Are there any questions?"

After a short silence, Richard Anders dismissed the class, quickly going back to the papers carelessly strewn about he had left only minutes before. Students jumped up, anxious to file out and explore the eateries and student hangouts that dotted the campus and beyond.

"How about that coke?"

Jeb Westfield was nothing if not persistent. I buckled and agreed.

"I know a great place just off campus. Are you up for a long walk?"

"Of course. It's a great day for a walk."

"Good. How about if you tell me your name as we go. We haven't really been properly introduced."

"Annie May Parker. I'm from a small town not far from here. I'm a day student."

"I live off campus, too. I live in an apartment in the city with a couple of buddies from my days in Westchester County.

"We're headed for a small restaurant around the corner from campus called Jeremiah's. The students pile in until closing time. It's cramped but casual. I think you'll like it."

Jeb attempted to slow his loping strides to match mine but it was me who had to catch up. "What are you taking?"

"I'm planning to be an English major. I would like to teach."

"A noble ambition. I'm in engineering. I'm here to learn the tech part so I can get my dad's company back for him. He's a nice, mild guy who just happened to have a good idea and got taken advantage of by a giant firm with a lot of nerve and no ethics."

"He must be very proud of you."

"I don't know. I'm pretty brash and he's tried to tone me down but it hasn't worked.

"We're almost to Jeremiah's. You can really keep up for a girl."

"We're tough where I come from. I'm here to make it and I'm not going to let a short hike keep me down."

"Good for you. Most girls fold at the first sign of trouble. I like your style.

"We're here."

At that, Jeb took my arm and pulled me into Jeremiah's, already filled with students cramming up to the counter and shouting orders at a heavy-set man with a soiled white apron and a hamburger flipper in his hand. He was flipping hamburgers as fast as he could on a very used grill and mixing sodas and sundaes while the ground beef sizzled behind him.

"Hey, Jeremiah, how about a couple of burgers and cokes?"

"You'll have to wait your turn, Jeb. Settle down and

I'll have them over to you at that table in the corner. It looks like somebody's leaving."

Jeb rushed over and grabbed the table, motioning me to join him. "Hey, Annie May, get over here before we get trampled.

"Jeremiah's an ex-marine but he's got a heart of gold. I came to Syracuse a few weeks ahead to get the apartment settled before Jackson and Ernie got here. I've hung out here just about every night for the last few weeks and become a regular. Jeremiah and I would talk into the night while I helped him close up. He's got a lot of stories to tell."

"He looks like a nice person."

"He is. Do you mind if I ordered for you?"

"A hamburger sounds great. I guess you could read my mind. First day is a bit of a hassle."

"You're right. One of Jeremiah's burgers is just the thing to get you settled into a new environment.

"So, tell me about yourself, Annie May."

I hesitated, but continued, assessing this boy who was so brash but so intense. "Nothing much to tell. I'm a simple farm girl who lives near the town of Baldwinsville in central New York, not far from here. My folks were farmers generations back. My father was a farmer with big ideas he never lived to see. We lost him to a threshing accident some years ago.

I have a sister at Wells College and a brother at home. I'm here to get an education so I can help out my family and follow my own dreams as well."

For the first time since I met him, Jeb was silent. Then, he spoke. "First, I'm sorry about your father.

"You're different, Annie May, than the girls I've known. They're all out for themselves. Oh, they all know how to dress and look like a million bucks but there's nothing inside.

"I wish you a lot of luck here." At that, our hamburgers and cokes arrived and Jeb became busy bantering with Jeremiah, his brash demeanor returning.

As Jeremiah returned to his grill, Jeb turned to me. "You're far from simple, Annie May.

"I propose a toast." He raised his coke. "To Syracuse and us. May we be great together."

As we finished our hamburgers Jeb bade a hasty goodbye to Jeremiah and we headed back to campus. "Gotta catch a two P.M. psych class. I figure if I'm going to outmaneuver the firm that stole my dad's company I'm going to need a little help."

I smiled at Jeb's dedication to a strategy he had no idea would work. "I hope you have a lot of success."

"You too, Annie May. You deserve it."

As we parted company, Jeb to his psychology class, me to an American history lecture I already felt I lived, Jeb took my number and promised to call with the hope we could start a study club.

"Sounds great. That's what I'm here for."

As I drove back home at the end of the day, the sun a brilliant, golden orb sinking into shades of red and mauve, I thought of the wonders the books I would study must hold and the secrets their authors held so tightly. Then, as the stars began to appear in a steadily darkening sky, I turned my thoughts to guessing what aroma would waft through the kitchen windows left open to catch the soft night breezes as I turned off the key in the truck and parked it safely in the old barn. As I turned the last corner, the lights of home visible in the distance, the weariness of the day settling in, I searched for the brightest star in the sky and wished upon it.

Chapter Twenty-Five

By November, with the snow and the ice of upstate New York swirling about me on the Syracuse campus I had adjusted to college life but not to the whirl of the social scene. I had dated some, but none of the boys seemed my type.

Most of the girls I saw at the few parties I attended wore heavy makeup and clothes that were obviously purchased in the upscale shops of Manhattan. Although Hank Peterson still gave me the pick of the new fashions that came in, his taste was more down home than urban.

Without Carrie, I was all thumbs in applying makeup of any sort and the girls who I met during gabfests after hours and who kindly offered to help me learn the art and the tricks of eye liner and lip gloss lost my interest only a few minutes into our well-meaning sessions.

I decided to knuckle down to the books as a way of coping. I soon became an expert in study habits and despite my off-campus status was sought after by the many elite who knew the names of every debutante who had come out that season but couldn't cite the name of one great author, give a run-down on the U.S. Constitution, or even give a clear answer as to why Alfred Nobel set up the prize he did.

Richard Anders' class was as much fun as he had proposed. We read excerpts from writings around the world and wrote essays on them. Jeb and I drew funny pictures about each and every one and occasionally when we were close to the brink of overtired late at night in his apartment surrounded by our study club group we wrote skits and one-act plays presenting them to the delight of our overtired study charges.

Richard Anders had also honored me with a request to fill the post of his research assistant for a grant he had received to launch a career in fiction writing. I spent many late nights filing his papers and putting them in order, a task he had never taken to. I also spent many hours at the Carnegie Library looking up details from how many spots a leopard has to how a whippoorwill makes his calls.

Our study club was gaining ground on campus and our reputation for late nights along with it. As I got up to leave a particularly intense American history lecture I was approached by a very thin and somewhat bedraggled girl, pale cheeks and mousy brown hair, but with a determined look in her deep, brown eyes with the typical student dark circles beneath them.

"Excuse me, are you Annie May Parker?"

"Yes, I am."

"I hear you have the best study group on campus."

"Well, thanks."

"I'm Josie Morton. Would you have room for me in it?"

"I think so. We always have room for more.

"How about if we go for coffee and discuss it. I'd like to get out of this crowd."

At that, some color came into her cheeks and she perked up. "Thanks. I'd like that."

As we trudged along the quad toward a small café I had mentioned, we were silent, our own thoughts swirling about in our heads, the leaves of the trees falling gracefully every now and then, hitting the ground, baring the branches, and suggesting the winter ahead.

We entered the café and found a small table at the back, ordering coffee and two small pastries which arrived before the crowd pressed in and cleaned out the café's daily cache. We sat as our coffee cooled before us.

"What brings you to Syracuse, Josie?"

"I'm here to get an engineering degree. I'm the only girl in my class."

"Well, it must get a little bit lonely at times. I give you a lot of credit. It's hard to get in and break that mold."

"The boys do keep to themselves. But, I don't care. I get most of my information from books anyway.

"My problem is I like history more than engineering. But, my parents said that history doesn't lead to a career and engineering does. I'm from Iowa and they're very practical there.

"My Uncle Charlie is an engineer at General Electric in Syracuse and they thought he could watch over me while I'm here. But, he has little time for me since he's involved in research and development and can only think about the next invention and patent and stays late nights at the lab.

"His wife is nice, but they have a passel of kids and she doesn't have much time for me."

"I looked at Josie, her pale demeanor much like a delicate bird, and spoke. "My friend Jeb is an engineering major and his roommate Ernie a history major with plans to go to law school. Their third roommate Jackson, a preppie type but a serious pre-med, is a science buff. I think they could all be helpful to you."

"Thanks, Annie May. I'm kind of shy with boys but I think I can make it."

"Well, I'm sure they'll fix that. They are none of them shy. In fact, they have complaints on a daily basis from their landlord who threatens them regularly with eviction. But, they manage to charm him out of it.

"I need to get back to classes. Would you care to walk with me?"

"Sure. I have one more myself."

As we crisscrossed the quad, Josie talked non-stop about her family and their farm. She had one older brother who had fled farm life for the city and who she missed dearly. Her folks were strict but kind-hearted and desperately wanted a better life for their daughter. "My father has struggled with making ends meet ever since I can remember. He has no knack for farming but he has a diligence to support his family. He was thrown into despair when Kenneth left for the city and still hopes he will return. But, Kenny is firm. He has no taste for farming."

"I'm sure they're proud of you."

"Well, everything's falling on me now and I'm not sure I'm up to it."

"We're still new here. I'm sure you'll find your way."

"Thanks, Annie May. You seem to have it all together."

"My older sister has been the flighty one so I always had to be the responsible one and somehow it stuck. But, I think I can follow my dreams at the same time. It just takes a little effort.

"I hope you can come for supper some time. Mama loves to cook and now that Carrie is away I know she'd like the extra company."

"I'd like that. I'm pretty good on a tractor so perhaps I could help out at planting time."

"My Uncle John thinks girls get in the way but he's a soft touch when it comes right down to it. I know he could use the help, at least for an afternoon.

"Well, here's my building. If you show up at the address I gave you on Wednesday evening, we can get a start on working you into the study club."

As Josie shuffled on to her own class I thought of how much alike we were in many ways. I hoped for her success and despite her shyness I somehow knew she'd find it. She had a determination that wouldn't quit.

As I found a seat in the statistics lecture, a class I despised but my advisor had insisted I take to fill a requirement, I thought of the winter coming on. I would take Georgie shopping in town for a snowsuit. He must have grown at least a foot since last Christmas. I would check his sled and repair all the scrapes and round up Jester so the three of us could go sledding on Strawberry Hill, make angels in the snow, and build a snowman as high as the barn with charcoal eyes, a carrot nose, and proper charcoal buttons causing Jester to run in circles around this curious newcomer while barking with delight.

I pulled out my notebook, and a pen I kept handy for the occasion. I was prepared to keep up with the rapid pace of Professor Marsden and the speed he was noted for as his fingers held the chalk that flew over the large board behind him. As the sun streamed through the windows Professor Marsden tapped the podium, cleared his throat, and began his lecture.

Chapter Twenty-Six

The sturdy reddish-brown sandstone steps of the Brooklyn brownstone stoop that I sat on during the spring break of my sophomore year at Syracuse offered a view of the neighborhood and was a lovely entrance to the stately and gracious three-story building behind me. Children bicycled or roller skated over the concrete sidewalk below, played hide and seek or tag, some of them waving while trying to keep their balance or pleading with me to keep secret their obvious hiding place.

Jeb had invited me for spring break, and his parents had done their best to treat me like an honored guest. Jeb's mother Martha had gone out of her way to bring home the best pastries and chocolates Manhattan had to offer and sometimes the most wonderful meats and freshest fruits and vegetables from a Greenwich Village green grocer she was especially fond of.

They had treated me to the best view of New York they could. We had seen a Broadway play with lavish dances and beautiful melodies, had toured the Museum of Modern Art where Martha worked as a research assistant, viewing furniture exhibits that foretold the future, wooden sculptures that were flat, wavy and curvy, and paintings of misty, pastel hues of violet and pink that represented gardens and bridges. We had gone to the Metropolitan Museum of Art where we viewed beautiful and enchanting bowls, vases, urns and plates of the ancients and the deep and rich colors of so many European painters.

Jeb and I had eaten a hotdog purchased from a Manhattan street vendor and shared fluffy cheesecake with the most wonderful flavor in a famous restaurant called Lindy's. We walked the streets of Manhattan and acted silly, drawing not a single look or stare from the rushing passersby.

Martha was preparing a dinner of beef and country vegetables, a French provincial dish she was known for among her social set, and she had refused all help. I had come out to enjoy the brisk, evening air and to view the vagaries of a typical Brooklyn neighborhood. "A penny for your thoughts."

Jeb had joined me, his trademark grin in evidence, the evening gusts of wind ruffling his unruly tufts of hair. "I was just thinking how wonderful your parents have been to me. They have taken their time to show me New York, given me the use of a lovely guest room, and fed me the most wonderful food I have tasted outside of Mama's cooking. I feel like a queen."

"You should be treated like a queen. You're special Annie May.

"Mom and Dad have enjoyed having you here. They're New Yorkers through and through. They've never been on a farm or ever seen one up close. The nearest they've come to one is in a Grandma Moses painting. You've changed their idea of a farm girl. They were certain you would arrive with overalls and a pitchfork.

"Come on, I'll race you to the corner and you can see the real Brooklyn. Abby's Deli will be packed and Mrs. O'Malley around the corner who lives up over the pawn shop will be chasing her dog and cat and a large number of small children who will all be figuring out how to torment her next while she chases them yelling with a broom."

As we ran, the gusts of wind throwing off our pace, Jeb slowed to allow me to race past him, sending us into gales of laughter. As promised, Mrs. O'Malley was out chasing everyone who got in her way, and the windows along the narrow side street were open, letting in the fresh spring air and letting out the bickering and grievances of the day.

As we returned to the brownstone, sprinting at top pace and avoiding a number of marble games and tricycles, the aroma of Martha's casserole wafted about us, seeping through the cracks of the century-old front door and the windows slightly ajar, bringing a touch of France to the modest Brooklyn neighborhood. I rushed up the stairs hoping to be in time to set the table but Jeb's father Peter had already set out the china and the silver under Martha's capable supervision.

Martha was carrying a lovely pottery casserole to the side buffet and Peter was bringing a variety of drinks to set beside it. "You're just in time. Soup's on."

As we sat around the large mahogany dining table, Martha's favorite Beethoven sonata playing softly in the background, the conversation was lively and very much down to earth. Peter filled us in on his struggles of the day as an electrical engineer at a large Manhattan corporation where he was admired for his expertise but no longer owned the patents of his many brilliant inventions. Martha added her adventures in her attempt to track down a sculpture that was known to exist but had remained elusive to international museum staffs for years.

For dessert, Martha flamed a brandied Cherries Jubilee alongside our table and dished it out in beautiful stemmed crystal. As we finished, she suggested Jeb and Peter, who were already lost in conversation, move to the study while we "girls" did the dishes.

The kitchen was large and well-appointed, with the latest in appliances and the most modern décor. But, in the corner stood a glassed in cabinet which held a number of antiques, a nod to the ancient brownstone we were standing in.

Martha pulled two aprons from a cabinet, both with modern art stamped all over them, and handed one to me. "These are left over from the museum's charity auction. But, the antiques in the corner were handed down to me from my mother. She ran an antiques store in the Village and I grew up there. These are all I have left to remember her by. These, and the beautiful memories of how much she valued and loved antiques."

"They are beautiful, Martha."

"Thank you, Annie May. May I ask you a question?"

"Of course."

"Are you and Jeb dating?"

"We're friends. We've been friends since freshman year. Jeb's enthusiasm has brought fun to the doldrums of college life, especially before exams and finals. But, he's a serious student."

"Well, I sometimes think his enthusiasm might get him into trouble. He's pretty forthright. I just think the right girl might settle him down."

"Jeb's very popular. He's dated a lot, but he just hasn't found the right girl."

"I hope he finds one like you, Annie May. You seem to be very responsible."

"I think Jeb will settle down when he's ready. Jeb is brash but he's very reliable. I think he just wants to make the right decision."

"Thanks for talking to me. I know it's difficult, but Jeb's not very forthcoming on his personal life. And, I don't want to pry.

"Now, I think we better tackle these dishes. Jeb and Peter could stay up all night talking engineering."

As I headed back home at the end of the week, the glow and excitement of Manhattan still swirling about me, the warmth of Brooklyn, despite the variety of cultures and architecture, still clinging, I thought of the year ahead. Jeb was closer to his goal but I was a question mark in my own mind. Carrie and Will were both certain of their future.

I decided to count the small towns I passed to keep myself awake and keep my fingers crossed that I would beat the rainstorm threatening in the sky above. Thunder claps echoed in the distance and as they neared I prepared myself for the decibels of thunder, the crackling of lightning bolts, and the eventual downpour that would be sure to follow.

I tossed my ideas for my history paper about in my head. It was due the first day of classes after the spring break and I knew I would be staying up all night to write it. I fished in my bag that sat on the seat next to me for the miniature farm I had found for Georgie in a quirky gift shop in the Village. I made up a story for the entire farm family the artist had depicted and for all the animals in the barn. Before I knew it, I had passed through town, the shops all closed, Hank Peterson's dry goods lit up but empty save for Golden Boy, his loyal calico cat, and I was rounding the corner toward home.

Chapter Twenty-Seven

The buttercups were already sprouting in the meadows and spring was turning into an early summer as Josie and I headed for home to spend the weekend studying for final exams. Josie had morphed from a shy Iowa farm girl into an easterner look-alike, thanks to the highlights her Manhattan roommates pulled through her light brown hair and the contacts she exchanged for the horn-rimmed glasses she had arrived with.

But, Josie hadn't strayed far from her roots. She was a favorite of Mama's and Georgie's, who trusted her with decisions on new crops to plant, and Uncle John had bent his rules on girls and farming and had included her in planting time. Josie couldn't wait to feel the sun on her back and the tractor beneath her as she sowed the new seeds and nurtured them as they grew.

As we pulled into the driveway we were greeted with the aroma of a baked ham studded with cloves and a pan full of fried potatoes. An apple pie sat cooling on the window sill. Mama was bustling about, her apron full of the remains of the squash she was preparing to mash, and Georgie was setting the table. Josie raced in to hug them both, promising Georgie she would race him in the meadows after the supper dishes were dried and put away.

Supper was set and we all sat down, Josie and I weary from study and anxious to dig in to the bounty of farm life after days and days of campus burgers and all-nighters. "How are your parents, Josie?"

"Fine, Mrs. Parker. I know Mother is anxious to try the recipes you sent."

"Well, I had extra copies and I thought I could share our New York know-how with Iowa. Your mother was kind enough to share her recipe for a wonderful rhubarb pie I thought had gone out of style. The men on this farm couldn't get enough of it."

"I know Mother is glad for your letters and letting her know how I'm doing here. I know I don't write as often as I should and I know she gets anxious even though she doesn't let on."

"How is your father doing with the farm?"

"Mother and Father took Granny in last month so there's another mouth to feed. But, Granny has won prizes for her canning so they're adding jams and jellies to their roadside stand come summer.

"Father has perked up with a friend of Kenny's from town who's shown an interest in farming. Father's been giving him lessons on tractor mechanics and hopes to start him spreading seed come planting time.

"He hopes that Simon's interest will lure Kenny back to the farm. But, Kenny is firm. He has a big job in marketing for a company in Des Moines and won't give that up. But, he has agreed to bring his newly found know-how to the farm come harvest time.

"There will be a clash between the old and the new. Father doesn't change easily, but I think Kenny can handle it. Kenny is certain that Father is stuck in another century and Father thinks what he calls 'these new-fangled ways' are nothing but trouble."

Josie paused, then turned to Georgie. "How's the math coming now that I showed you those shortcuts?"

"Well, Mrs. Hazelton thinks I'm smart and I can finish my homework in half the time and spend the rest of the time looking over the new seed catalogues."

"School is hard. But, you'll like knowing the math when you figure out how much seed you need and how much profit you can make and counting the cash from your sales at the market. How about if I show you how to set up a roadside stand?"

"Would you, Josie? I'd really like that. I've always wanted one. Then, I can sell right here. Papa was always going to show me but he never got around to it."

Mama answered. "Papa was always going to do a lot of things and he had big dreams. But, he never got the time to do them all.

"Georgie, how about finishing up and Josie can fill in for you as the dish dryer while you go up and do your homework."

A groan from Georgie was not enough to change Mama's mind. Georgie went upstairs while we three did the dishes and Mama caught up on our college struggles.

"Are you girls eating right?"

"Yes, but not as well as here, Mama. No eatery on campus can take the place of your cooking,"

"Annie May, you stop flattering me. If there's something you want, you just come out with it."

"I think I might want to take back some of your cherry pie. I've been telling almost everyone on campus how you've won the prize at the state fair since I can remember. They've been begging for a taste ever since."

"Well, I thought I'd send some back with you. And, maybe a pan of Josie's favorite butterscotch brownies with chocolate chips."

"Thanks, Mama. I know that will make me the most popular student on campus."

"What are you girls learning in school?"

"We're both learning a lot of American history. Josie's learning all kinds of science and I'm studying books in English and struggling with a course in statistics which I don't understand or I guess care to."

"I had classes I didn't understand at Baldwinsville High but I tried my best. Learning's a hard thing, but it pays in the end.

"Papa was better at it than I was. He had a thirst for learning. He didn't mind spending time poring over those old books on farming he found in his folks' attic. Many nights he spent by the fire sighing and dreaming, puffing on one of his old pipes and laying out a design in his head for a farm he was going to call High Point Acres.

"He even had a plan to feed all the hungry people

who were starving in the world. Papa was a dreamer alright."

"He sounds like a wonderful person, Mrs. Parker."

"He was, Josie. And, I know he would have been proud of you girls. He used to say to me, 'Marylee, we better treat those little tads right, because they're going to take over the world one day. And, they better know what they're doing because that's all they'll have'.

"Now, that should be the last of the cleanup and I'll put the dishes away while you girls get down to your studies. There's a new program on the radio that plays all the old music from the twenties so I can listen while I finish up the hem on Carrie's new skirt I've been working on for spring. Carrie's travelling in some high circles with Jamie so she needs to look right."

"Okay, Mama, we'll get out of your way and get down to the books. Supper was scrumptious."

"It was, Mrs. Parker. It always makes me think of home."

"You say 'hello' to your folks when you write them next."

"I will."

Josie raced Georgie in the meadow as promised and then traded silly stories before his bedtime. As we sat down to study, Josie paused. "Do you think Jeb's roommate Jackson will ever ask me out?"

"Jackson's shy and he's bent on getting to medical school. He doesn't date much."

"What does a girl have to do to get his attention?"

"He likes music. Why don't you get him a Tommy Dorsey record? He got up at dawn to get the best seats for the Dorsey concert when the band came to campus last fall."

"Okay. Maybe that would work. I know a great record shop near campus. Will you help me pick it out?"

"Of course. But, I think you better be careful setting your sights on Jackson. His family is part of the Long Island horsey set and they're very careful who they let in."

"But, he's so dreamy. He's all I think about all day. Tall, perfectly groomed blond hair, with the most impeccable gentlemanly manner. I can't get him off of my mind."

"Okay, but he does come with a word of warning. He's not very sensitive when it comes to his friendships going sour. Jeb's had to bail him out a number of times."

"I'll take note. I just can't wait to get back to campus and see if the Dorsey record works."

"I'll keep my fingers crossed. Jackson's a good catch. He's serious but he's fun when he lets down. He and Jeb have closed up most of the student hangouts on campus and off. But, we better get down to the books. Professor Hayes is known for his hard finals."

As the moonlight pored through the open windows, we tried to make sense of wars and presidents and people who had the courage and the foresight to found a country out of a vast and sometimes confounding wilderness, building it into the great power it was destined to become.

Weary at midnight, we packed up the books and slid under the clean sheets Mama had ironed especially for our arrival. Josie was asleep in Carrie's bed before we could say goodnight. I turned off the lights and left the shade up, counting the stars and admiring the bright full moon. The sun would be up soon enough and we would be heading back to campus for a final round of tests and the end of another semester. Hank Peterson had given me a standing invitation for a job in his dry goods store every summer for as long as I wanted. I began to count piles of sweaters and tee shirts in my head as I promptly fell asleep.

Chapter Twenty-Eight

Exams were over and summer was in full swing when Carrie arrived home with a bundle of fashion projects she had completed and plans for a June wedding the following year. Jamie had presented her with a diamond the size of which we had never seen before. If diamonds were shown at the state fair, this one would have won the grand prize. But it was tasteful as well, because Carrie would have accepted none other.

She and Jamie had decided on a wedding the following year immediately after their graduations. Carrie was walking on air and was full of wedding plans in her head. Mama was so happy for her and would do anything to please Jamie and his family and Carrie as well. But, she had ideas of her own she had harbored for years,

As for me, I stewed silently, torn between good wishes for Carrie and the thought that, despite the fact that I liked Jamie, I was about to lose my only sister to him. I mostly puttered about, trying to stay out of the way for fear my thoughts would be discovered.

Carrie, back at Sandler's Drugs for the summer, was enjoying the attention her engagement ring was getting as she served sodas and sundaes at the lunch counter. Every teenaged girl swooned over the size of her diamond and made bets with her friends as to who would net the biggest catch in the future.

The elders of the town were less taken by Carrie's good fortune. Mrs. Addison, in for her weekly medications, clucked when she saw the size of Carrie's diamond. "Don't get too uppity, Carolyn Parker. And, don't forget where you came from."

Carrie took it all in stride, writing Jamie every day and counting the days until his family opened their summer place at the edge of town.

Will was home as well, working the farm with Uncle John, romping with Jester, and jumping in the usual swimming holes with Georgie when they got a chance. But, this year was different. Will was more serious than usual, and much more distant. I tossed it off to his maturing and the toll it took to become a serious college student.

I decided to test out my theory on a very hot June day. As Will rounded the corner on the tractor Uncle John had spent most of the spring tuning up, I drenched him with a pitcher of ice cold water I had prepared specifically for that purpose. "Okay, Annie May, I'll get you as soon as I finish fertilizing the fields. You'll regret taking advantage of a poor farm hand."

"You're far from a poor farm hand, Will Vanderwort. I heard you got into vet school."

"News travels fast. I got in on early admission.

"And, what about you? You're going to be a junior. You should be getting a start on becoming famous already. I hear you're in some pretty heavy literary circles there. I've got a buddy who dates a Syracuse girl. He's on your campus just about every weekend.

"If we call a truce, I'll catch up with you later. How about Strawberry Hill at four o'clock? "

Four o' clock was the perfect time to head for Strawberry Hill. I had finished my hours at Hank Peterson's and I had in mind to help Mama with supper by mixing some biscuits to go with the ham she was preparing to make. The sun was lowering in the sky and the hues of the meadow flowers were still brilliant despite the shadows.

Will was there already when I arrived, sitting near the top surveying the fields, the meadows, and part of the Taylor farm, the haze of the horizon a far distance beneath the clear blue sky. I joined him at his chosen spot.

"Well, I see you haven't lost your hiking skills getting soft on that Syracuse campus."

"I could still beat you back to the house if I had a mind to."

"I thought you would lose that by now. From what I can see the college boys like the clingy, swoony type."

"I haven't had too much time to date. With being a day student and a job on campus and Saturdays in town, and what with hitting the books I haven't had too much time left over. What about you? I'm surprised some clingy college girl hasn't nabbed you already."

"I have a job in one of the dorms doing maintenance to pay for my room and board and it has been nearly a full-time job doubling up on my courses to gain early admission and save a year's tuition."

"I knew you could do it. And, you'll be that much closer to being a vet."

"I can't wait. There's so much I want to do. There's so much new research and there's so much I want to contribute. They're on the edge of finding a cure for so many diseases that level the herds and wipe out the horse populations."

"I know you'll be sought after, Will. The animals look up to you already. You've saved so many cats and dogs and I know the Taylor horses are grateful for tracking down the disease that plagued them last summer.

"And, I see the way Jester looks at you. You won't have any problem with people bringing their pets to you."

"I'm not sure what I want to do. Research looks good. But, it's a few years away so I have time to think about it.

"It looks like you have kept safe the likeness of Gullinbursti I carved and trusted you with when I first went away. The farm is doing great. Your Uncle John has added a number of modern methods to the fertilizing and the planting. And, he's teaching Georgie a lot of them and giving him more responsibility."

"I have kept your carving of Gullinbursti in a very safe place and he has watched over the farm these past few years like you said. I think his magical powers have worked."

"And, what about your plans, Annie May? Are you going to become a famous writer?"

"I would rather help create writers and readers. I so much want to teach. But, before I do I want to soak up everything I can. Syracuse has a great department for that and I'm lucky I have a job with Richard Anders. I've learned so much from Richard and his friends."

"Your students will be lucky. You'll be steeped in knowledge by then.

"Now, enough of this serious talk. I'll race you back to the barn. And, then I'll show you some robin's eggs in a nest I discovered attached to the hayloft. It's late for roosting, but I think we can get a look before they hatch."

Will plucked a daisy and put it in my hair. "You can save it for when you find a fella to love."

"That's going to be a while. It looks like I'm in for getting a masters."

The eggs were still in the nest, the beautiful blue still a wonder as they lay cradled in the twigs of a carefully crafted home site.

As Will headed for home, I studied the sunset, idly ticking off the many shades of mauves and pinks that crowded the sky. I made a mental note to round

Georgie up from the roadside stand he had made with the help of Josie, and where he spent many hours showcasing the fruits of his labors, and to save some supper for Carrie when she returned at ten dished from serving sodas and sundaes to the late night crowd at Sandler's.

I entered the kitchen, pulling the big crockery mixing bowl from its place on the highest shelf. I mixed up a batch of biscuits while the aroma of baked ham studded with cloves and laid with pineapple filled the room and wafted out through the screens of the open windows toward the gentle breezes of a very warm summer evening.

Chapter Twenty-Nine

C arrie and I waded through the tall, thick grasses of the meadows, the deep pink red buds of the wood roses and the perfect pink of the blossoms in bloom all around us, as we headed out to pick berries from the berry patches that studded Strawberry Hill and rhubarb from the patch Mama had planted just this year aside the barn from crowns she had wheedled from Alma Taylor in exchange for some potted plants Alma had had her eye on. Mama was in the kitchen preparing a crust for a strawberry rhubarb pie she had found a recipe for in one of the glossy magazines she relied on that held menus for special occasions that promised to impress your guests and perhaps even make you the talk of your social circles as she worked to prepare a Sunday dinner for Pastor Ezekiel Brown and his family whose invitation to today's dinner she had wangled almost a year ahead from the president of the ladies' church group.

Pastor Brown, or "Zeke" as he was known to his younger parishioners, was a replacement for Reverend Morton who had retired due to ill health and a rebel escaped from the pressures of urban congregations. Although his annual salary in Pottersville was less than his former urban flocks were able to pay, he was well fed by the ladies of Pottersville who brought him chickens and eggs, roasts and pies, and vegetables and fruits of all kinds handpicked at harvest time and then canned for the winter season.

Pastor Brown's wife, Elizabeth, as small and quiet as he was big and brawny, was a good addition to the Pottersville church, joining the ladies' group, and knitting mittens and socks for the poorer children of Pottersville and the poverty pockets of Syracuse. Their children, very young, and very close in age, were models of good behavior.

As we trekked through tangles of meadow grasses, stopped only by a squirrel or two, or a rabbit running scared and zig zagging in search of its meadow home, Carrie was uncharacteristically silent. "Hey, Squirrel, what happened to the gossip? You must have plenty to tell working at Sandler's Drugs."

"I do. Especially about the feud that's going on between Mr. Sandler and old Mrs. Abernathy who's certain that Mr. Sandler has been cheating her and replacing her medications with pills of the wrong color since her mind has gone and her son hasn't taken the time to get her to a doctor in Syracuse.

"But, all I can think of is my wedding. What color the bridesmaids dresses, what flowers to deck the church with, what flowers to carry, who should have corsages and boutonnieres and whether Jamie and I should write the oath or use the traditional standard. A lot of girls, and boys too, are writing their own these days."

"That's a lot to think about. But, more important, how are you and Jamie going to live? Where will you live? Have you settled all that yet?"

"I guess I just thought it would work itself out. It's a year away. But, I know Jamie wants to become a buyer in a big department store in New York. He just loves retail and wants someday to make his mark in it and rise to the top somehow."

"That's an ambitious goal. Jamie's bright and talented, so he'll most likely land there, but what about you?"

"I think I'll look for a job when the time comes, wherever we are. Mama's not happy that we won't be settling down here, but there's nothing for Jamie here to get him a start in his career. He has connections in New York and he intends to use them.

"But, I told Mama we would visit as often as we could. Jamie's folks have promised him a car for graduation, so we can make it on Jamie's days off. There should be plenty of opportunity for that and he loves it here, especially in the summer when his folks open their summer home."

"What about Georgie? He's been so quiet lately, hanging his head and looking sad when he thinks no one is watching."

"I guess I've been so busy planning my wedding I haven't noticed. I think I'll take Georgie into Mayberry on Saturday. There's a western playing at the new movie house and we can stop in at Sandler's back in town for a double chocolate soda."

"I think he'd like that. As for me, who will I gossip with at night, or on lazy Sunday afternoons on Strawberry Hill?

"Annie May, I know I've been selfish and only thinking of myself in all this excitement, but we will always be sisters. I promise I will write often, and you will be the first to know every bit of gossip I can dig up on those New York socialites.

"Now, I guess we'd better start picking berries. Mama will be needing them for that pie she's baking for the new minister and his family. We can't let her down. She needs to best Mayva Williams whose trying to edge her out for a place on that new ladies' group committee."

Sunday dinner was a success, and Reverend Brown and his wife very appreciative. Pastor Brown had a large helping of the ham Mama had baked so slowly in the big old oven and had glazed with fresh pineapple, fresh cherries, scored by hand and studded so carefully with clove buds she had found in one of her catalogues imported from the Far East, and a second helping of the strawberry rhubarb pie.

"Marylee, I hear you're a great asset to the ladies' group. Elizabeth was astonished at the number of mittens you turned in for the holidays. It's a lot of work to run this farm. We're very appreciative."

"I have a lot of help with the farm in my brother-in-law John Turner. He's seen to it that the farm runs as smoothly as it can after we lost Tyler.

"Tyler was a church-going man, Reverend. He couldn't always get there for Sunday service but he believed there was a special power that brought round the harvest besides the long hours of labor he spent and the many hours of reading he did to keep up with the many new advances."

"You have served his memory well, Marylee. You have a beautiful place here and a very special family. I hear you will be tying the knot, Caroline. When is the big day?"

"Next June, Pastor. We have so many details to plan before the big day."

"If you and your young man ever need to seek my council I will be there to hear you. Marriage is a big step."

"I appreciate that.

"And John George, will you be taking over the farm when you come of age?"

"I would like to. Uncle John says I'm a natural."

"Well, good for you. And, Anabel May, what do you choose to do?"

"Right now I'm studying English literature at Syracuse. I hope to teach."

"The world always needs good teachers. It's a noble vocation.

"And now, it's time to stretch after such a wonderful meal. I know Elizabeth will want to help the ladies clean up. Maybe John George could help me with the young ones and give us a tour of this wonderful farm. I know besides taking a ride on the tractor they've had their eye on the tire swing out back."

Elizabeth Brown was a delight. She not only helped Mama, she talked wedding colors with Carrie and was a whiz in the history of English literature.

Georgie gave tractor rides to the little ones, pushed them on the tire swing, played tag and hide and seek, always letting them win. Reverend Brown showed them a game of touch tag played with a ball that he had learned in divinity school.

It was plain to see that Mama was a shoo-in for the spot on the ladies' committee.

As the Browns said their goodbyes, thanking Mama profusely and murmuring encouraging words to the rest of us, I looked at Mama. The lines that had begun to form on her face had become more deeply etched and her hair was losing its beautiful chestnut color with strands of gray. But, the glow on her face was unmistakable.

As Carrie and I settled in for the night after a round of board games with Georgie, we exchanged our usual gossip, Carrie's from Sandler's Drugs and mine overheard in the dressing rooms of Peterson's Dry Goods. The night was hot and sticky, no breeze from the open window, but the beams of a full moon shone through and dimly lit our room with a soft, silvery blue.

I lay on top of the covers hoping for a breeze to come up. With tomorrow an early morning at Sandler's, Carrie was sound asleep.

Chapter Thirty

The following summer was a hot one according to the records of Onondaga County and was filled with flurry and excitement. Georgie graduated from high school and Carrie and Jamie from college.

Kinfolk came from all over, some who we hadn't seen for years, and some who had kept in touch with Christmas cards and notices of baptisms.

Tents were pitched in meadows and campers parked in campgrounds near Mayberry. Mama and Aunt Maybelle had been freezing tiny sandwiches for months and the ladies of the church group had come round mixing salads and slaws, baking beans, and bringing cakes and pies, and cookies of all kinds.

Georgie and Uncle John dug a pit and lined it with stones for cooking hams and roasts and fish caught in the streams that ran out back behind the town and roasting marshmallows on spits after dark.

Carrie's wedding followed graduation and most of the guests stayed on to celebrate and wish Carrie and Jamie well. Friends of Jamie's folks arrived, filling hotels in the larger cities around.

Carrie was a beautiful bride and Reverend Brown performed a beautiful ceremony. Orchids filled the church, thanks to Jamie's mother and her careful tending of the greenhouse attached to their summer place at the edge of town.

Max was best man and Georgie an usher with me as the only attendant to Carrie. Mama had spent most of the spring sewing our dresses following Carrie's design and had made her own, a green silk that took her fancy when Hank Peterson gave her first dibs on the newest bolts that arrived in early spring from New York.

The wedding was Carrie's idea of a compromise with Mama. Carrie had insisted on a church wedding and Mama had carried visions of Carrie as a bride in our parlor or outside if the weather was sunny.

All of our kinfolk who had known Papa walked up the aisle with Georgie insisting he had grown to be a spitting image. Those who were friends of Jamie's family were certain that everyone who filled the church was quaint.

Will arrived in a summer linen suit, his home haircuts from his early years traded in for the posh trim of a Mayberry barber. I was certain all of Carrie's classmates who were guests at the wedding would be vying for his attentions immediately after the ceremony.

Josie arrived as well, looking slender and lovely in a turquoise blue silk dress, her eyes still looking red and swollen from a breakup with Jackson who buckled to a threat by his parents who promised to disinherit him if he didn't drop her and find a more appropriate choice from their social set.

"Hey, Annie May, what made you turn in your tomboy outfits for high fashion?"

"You don't look so bad yourself, Will. I see the overalls are gone."

"I just squeaked back for the wedding. I'm staying on for a few weeks as a research assistant. One of my profs asked me to do the detail work for a paper he's presenting in Austria. It's a great chance to get a start and learn about techniques and the latest in discoveries around the world."

"That's exciting. We'll miss you on the farm."

"I'll be back in July. Georgie should be running things along with your Uncle John by then. He's a new graduate and I hear he's going to be a full-time farmer."

"Yes, he's firm about that. Mama is a tad bit disappointed because she wanted us all to go to college. But, Georgie can't wait to get a start in farming. He has a bundle of big ideas."

"He's a good farmer, Annie May. He beat out everybody at the market in sales when he was only thirteen. And, he has great ideas on how to rotate the crops and how to get the most yield for the money."

At that, Alison Jones, the church organist hired for the occasion, began to play and everyone scurried for their seats. I walked up the aisle with Georgie, proud as could be, to take my place next to Jamie and Max. A hush fell as everyone waited for Carrie to make her entrance.

Alison Jones broke the silence with a rousing "Here Comes the Bride" and Carrie entered, erect and steady on Georgie's arm. Gasps arose as the guests stood to get a better look.

Carrie's dress was a vision, a beautiful satin covered with delicate seed pearls, a large satin bow in the back beneath the tiny little buttons, and a veil of French silk tulle uncovered in a search of an enormous Rochester fabric store. Whispers rose immediately from the Manhattanites that it was surely a Coco Chanel.

I didn't have to look at Mama to know the pride she was feeling. Her eyes were full of tears as Carrie and Georgie reached the altar. I remembered to take the spot I had been assigned so Carrie could take her place beside Jamie and recite her vows.

Both Carrie and Jamie had written their own vows, a step that had not as yet been taken in the small church of Pottersville, but Reverend Brown was happy to insert them into the ceremony. I had secretly been enlisted to help Carrie with hers and Jamie was glowing with anticipation to hear them read before the crowd of parishioners and his Manhattan guests.

Max had the rings and Emma, Aunt Maybelle's youngest, was flower girl intent upon keeping Carrie's train from dragging along the floor. The ceremony went fast, and Reverend Brown departed slightly from the usual patter to inject his own words of wisdom.

As Carrie and Jamie walked back down the aisle glowing with excitement and happiness there were tears in the eyes of many of the guests, even the most hardened from New York. As they exited the church to wait outdoors, the rest of us filed out into the sunlight greeted cordially by Pastor Brown standing in the doorway to the organ playing of Alison Jones who had changed the beat of the music to match the tempo of the jazz she dearly loved and jammed with until all hours of the night with like-minded friends who filled her tiny house set back in the middle of the village.

The reception, held at home at Mama's request, was a continuation of the graduation celebration, and lasted well into the night. Carrie and Jamie joined us for a few hours until they left for New York and a short honeymoon at a seaside resort on the New Jersey shore, a gift of Jamie's parents.

As I carried platters of small sandwiches and refilled bowls of slaw, Max found me. "Annie May, it's so nice to see you. It seems like it's been forever since we shared a spring weekend and I was a social clod."

"I didn't think you were a clod, just a freshman getting used to college life. I felt very honored that you shared with me your favorite clearing off the beaten path of the Harvard Yard. There was so much peace there. I enjoyed our talk."

"Thanks to our talk I switched my major. I went after what I wanted instead of what the generations assumed I'd follow. I have a double major in history and government. I'll be getting a masters and plan to go into politics, for better or worse."

"I'm so glad, Max. You have a gift and I'm glad you will be sharing it with the citizens of this country."

"Thanks, Annie May. I have you to thank for encouraging me to follow my dreams and to stand up for what I think. No girl ever believed in me before. I will never forget your help. And, I wish you all the luck in the world in whatever you do."

"I am planning on teaching. One more year to go and then a masters."

"You'll make a great teacher."

Max turned to go, but thought better of it, blushed and blurted out, "Annie May, is your friend Josie dating anyone in particular?"

"Not now, Max. She just broke up with someone. She's pretty delicate right now. I'm not sure she's interested."

"Well, I'd like to ask her out but I don't want to upset her."

"You can try. I'll put in a good word for you. She has a passion for history like you do. I think she would like getting to know you."

"Thanks, Annie May. Well, I think I better go do my job. Jamie and Carrie will be leaving soon and I want to propose another toast."

Carrie and Jamie left before sundown to make it to the New Jersey shore, and then, after their stay, to a seven floor walk-up in Brooklyn Jamie had found to fit the budget of two new college graduates. Jamie's graduation present, an old Dodge coupe, was fitted with a "just married" sign along the rear window and several tin cans and shoes tied neatly to the bumper, thanks to his college friends and several of the locals who were experts in the matter.

Mama held up as best she could in saying goodbye to Carrie, and Georgie and I did our best to bolster Mama. Carrie promised to call when they got there and to write as often as she could.

The celebration went on for hours after their departure. Most of the Manhattan guests had left after the ceremony, but those who stayed kept to themselves, clucking about the quaintness of the rural life they had never seen up close. But after a number of cups of Mama's punch, spiked with the spirits she liked best, they kicked off their heels, joined in the fun, sang as lustily as the rest of us around the campfire roasting marshmallows, and even joined the square dancing listening intently to the caller, and rooted for their favorites in the fiddling contest.

Will left early to get back to school and Max and Josie want off by themselves, engrossed in conversation. I looked up at the stars, bright as could be in a clear, dark sky. I was certain that those that were twinkling carried an omen for the future and the moon, which was nearly a full one, had a smile on the mythical creature inside it.

Chapter Thirty-One

I t was a grey day when I was called home by the news that Georgie had been drafted. The sky crackled all around with lightning and the thunder resounded through the halls, the classrooms and the secluded offices of campus buildings.

Richard Anders, who had been hired as assistant professor following his Ph.D. with honors, had agreed to be my advisor for my masters year. We were in conference when the guidance department reached me with the news.

I raced home, mindful of the wet roads and the tires on the truck that needed replacing. I would need to bolster both Mama and Georgie, despite the fact that I could use some comfort myself.

The conflict in Vietnam had escalated from a cold war alert, then a conflict, and then escalated again to an all-out war. The boys who had decided to work instead of attend college were all eligible for draft, and many of them were being called.

Georgie had made our fields sparkle, with wheat that blew when the winds were soft and gentle, and

266

corn that tasted of the freshness of all outdoors. His cabbages, tomatoes, beans and cucumbers consistently won first prize at the county fair, and he outsold everyone at the Mayberry Saturday market.

As I flew in the door, Georgie was standing in the kitchen holding the draft notice and Mama was sitting in the parlor trying to recover. I hugged Georgie and sat down next to Mama.

"Anabel May, I'm torn in how I feel. I believe everyone should do their duty by our country, but that conflict in Vietnam, now called a war. I don't know anyone who understands why we're even there."

"I know, Mama. I think Georgie is just as confused."

"Georgie has worked these fields into a model farm. He's just hitting his stride. And, he's so young to be going so far away from home. The other side of the world."

"We will make sure we send him everything we can to remember home. I will write him every day. And, I know Carrie will as well."

"I'm going to pack him some cookies to take along with him but he won't need any clothes. Everything will be army issue."

Georgie, still stunned, remained in the kitchen. I

walked in and hugged him once again. "Annie May, will you take care of Mama?"

"Of course I will. I gave up a bid for an exchange program at King's College in London to stay here with Mama. I'll write you every day. I know Mama will as well."

"I leave for Fort Dix in ten days for basic training. Then we ship out. It doesn't say where but it has to be Vietnam.

"Ethan Taylor and Jeb Oliver left about six months ago and have been stationed in Saigon. Maybe I'll run into them when I get there."

"Maybe you will, Georgie."

"I'll give instructions for the harvest to Uncle John. It has to be done just so to get the most yield."

"I know Uncle John will take good care of the farm. He's slowing down, but I know he doesn't want to quit. He says you're the best thing that happened to this farm."

"Uncle John taught me everything I know. Farming is in his lineage. I know he'll never give up.

I have to get back to the crops, they need dusting and fertilizing, but I'll come in as soon as the sun is low. I want to spend as much time as I can with Mama."

I watched Georgie, a boy on the brink of manhood, through the yellow chintz curtained windows climb up on the tractor he had tinkered with most of his life. I promised myself I would make his next days before departure as normal as I could.

I called Carrie who drove through the night from her Brooklyn walk-up to arrive by morning, bags under her eyes and sadly in need of a strong cup of coffee. I called Will, who left his lab job a few days later to arrive home and help Georgie dust and spray the crops.

Will took Georgie fishing, at the same time holding confabs on the future of the farm. Carrie took Georgie to the latest movie in Mayberry, a John Wayne cowboy thriller, complete with cattle rustling and sheep farmers, set against a background of beautiful western mountains. I played board games with him far into the night.

When the day of Georgie's departure arrived, we drove him to Rochester where the train was departing for Fort Dix. The station's grandeur belied the sadness we felt as we got him ready to board. As Georgie climbed aboard, kissing us and hugging us as if he didn't want to let go, we saw the same scene repeated in knots of families intermingled with business travelers and commuters.

With Will driving, me in the passenger seat, and Mama and Carrie in the back, we were as silent as could be on the trip back home. Carrie held her arms around Mama the whole way.

As Will left for school and Carrie for Brooklyn I felt the loneliness pervade what had once been a noisy and lively household. I made a mental note to be strong for Mama. She would need me more than ever now.

Chapter Thirty-Two

Spring brought the blossoms of the many cultivated plants to full bloom on the Syracuse campus. Josie and Jeb, both hearing the news of Georgie, formed a correspondence brigade, sending news of home and clipped cartoons from the campus newspaper, along with occasional care packages of super-sized chocolate chip cookies from Jeremiah's restaurant, where Jeb still often ate, and which Jeremiah baked himself. Jeb's upbeat humor was a first class hit with Georgie's unit, especially after they shipped out to Vietnam.

Both Jeb and Josie had plans set for after graduation. Jeb was planning to set up an engineering company with his father as CEO and himself as vice president of technical operations. He had already scouted the area in New Jersey and had found a suitable building which his father was bidding on right now.

Josie was planning to move to Boston to be near Max who had two more years of law school and with whom she was very nearly inseparable since they had met at Carrie's wedding. As we strolled across campus Josie rambled on about her plans, ignoring the horseplay of most of the students taken by spring fever and a desire for the semester to end. "Annie May, what do you think of my moving to Boston to be near Max?"

"Max is a good person. I think he's worth it."

"We're planning a summer wedding a year from now."

"I'm so happy for you. Have you met his family?"

"Max took me home right after we met. His folks were so cordial. Nothing like Jackson's family, even though they have the wealth to match. His mother took me shopping on Fifth Avenue and his father taught me croquet. They've even invited me along on a getaway to their camp in the Adirondacks which is very large with a lot of outbuildings and is staffed by servants but is still far from the hustle bustle of Manhattan and Long Island.

"We hit it off right away. They were so interested in farm work and what my folks were like. They even mentioned that if they had the time they would stop off to meet them on one of their many company trips."

"What will you do in Boston?"

"I found a cute little apartment near the Charles River not far from the university. I'll be working for a small farm equipment company designing new models of tractors and spreaders, and anything else I come up with, and in my spare time I'll be volunteering for the Massachusetts Historical Society. They just got a new bequest and they can't wait for me to catalogue it. They're swamped just keeping their vast permanent collection in order.

"What about you, Annie May?"

"I'll be substituting at Baldwinsville High and Mayberry Central until Mrs. Jenkins retires next spring. And, Richard's keeping me on as his assistant. I'll be researching his new novel and teaching a freshman class or two when he's away."

"And, what about a social life?"

"I'll be pretty busy just handling a work life."

"How about visiting Boston? Max has a lot of friends looking for dates who are tired of giddy coeds. There will be plenty of room to stay over in my apartment."

"I might just take you up on it. Right now I better get over to Richard's office. I'm sure he'll have piles of papers to correct and nowhere to turn. He's counting on his first novel to get his name out there and forge a career."

"You've been the strength for all of us, Annie May. I wish you so much luck. You deserve it."

As we parted ways, I thought how much Josie had changed since she came to Syracuse fresh from the fields of Iowa, scared of the future but not certain how to cope. I was sure she and Max together would change the world.

I thought of Georgie as well. I must remember to take some photographs of Jester catching a ball and chasing the barn cats. I would include some writing paper and some ball point pens. Georgie would be missing home.

The sun was taking its time sinking into the west. It was as if it wanted to stay and light my way. The mauves and pinks behind it were soft but the sun was striking in its brilliance. I picked up my pace and hurried on to Richard's. A bright student in the Pennsylvania coal mining town of his youth and a compelling and popular professor, he was lost without an assistant.

Chapter Thirty-Three

F all brought the most beautiful Indian summer weather along with falling leaves, reds, yellows and oranges, sent to the ground by gentle winds or more stronger ones during a sudden rainstorm. Mama spent a lot of time in the chrysanthemum bed cultivating the lush, dark soil or snipping old blooms.

I had received my masters without any fanfare except a congratulations from Richard and had said goodbye to both Jeb and Josie. Jeb promised to visit, especially if he was in the area on business which he expected to be, both in Rochester and Syracuse. Josie repeated her offer to visit Boston.

Carrie was expecting a baby in spring and promised a visit soon. Mama couldn't wait to pamper her and discuss her plans for a nursery.

Carrie arrived with most of the leaves still on the trees and weary from the long drive from Brooklyn. She collapsed quickly onto the sofa after hugging Mama and me.

Mama couldn't take her eyes off of Carrie, clucking about the remedies for morning sickness and making sure that Carrie ate well. "You're eating for two now, Carolyn Ann. You can't afford to eat like a bird."

"I know, Mama. The doctor instructed me and the nurse gave me a proper diet to follow. It's not like seeing old Doc Anderson here. New York offices are huge and are filled with all kinds of people doing all kinds of jobs."

"Doc Anderson has delivered hundreds of babies and he hasn't lost one."

"I might have to have him see to this one as well. Jamie is thinking of moving to Pottersville."

Mama gasped, and I, despite my cool demeanor, lost my verbal footing.

"Why so? I thought you and Jamie were doing so well in New York?

"We are, Mama. Jamie has risen to assistant buyer at Bloomingdale's in just two years and I have wangled a position part time as an assistant window dresser, along with my responsibilities in millinery.

"But, Jamie has bigger plans. He has always wanted to have a store of his own. And, with what he has learned at Bloomie's, he figures he's ready.

"When he was ten, he was given a toy department store complete with wooden figures of shoppers by a great-uncle who had risen in the ranks of both Macy's and Gimbels. He never stopped dreaming of having a store of his own."

"But why Pottersville? Hank Peterson already has a dry goods store and he's not ready to retire."

"Jamie has in his head an idea for a department store. It's a novel idea and lots of experts in the field have tried to talk him out of it. Department stores are built in large cities because that's where the largest number of buyers live. But, Jamie thinks that with the proper advertising buyers will come from the larger cities around if the store is special, if it has something none of the larger department stores in the cities can supply.

"And, it would bring up the economy of the town at the same time. He has always wanted to do something for Pottersville because his folks spent so many happy summers here. And, he knows how happy it would make me to move back home."

"Well, it might not work. Is Jamie willing to take that risk?"

"I believe in Jamie, Mama. He's smart and he's good. And, he says we are a team so he's certain it will work. He says if we can pull this off I will have my own fashion line, better than all the French and Italian houses combined.

"And, he doesn't intend to put Hank Peterson out of work. He would like to hire him to run a department just like his dry goods store. Jamie says too many companies overlook experience because they get drawn into the struggle of the daily politics that bring down a store."

"I think it's time to tend to the pot roast. Carolyn Ann, you get some sleep. Anabel May and I will fix supper. You need to eat."

As Mama bustled about in the kitchen, humming "Down By the Riverside," one of her favorites from her sing-along days, I pulled out the paring knife and set about to pare and core some of the apples I had pulled from the orchard behind the fields in a final harvest before the trees gave up their leaves to remain dormant for the winter. I would make an apple cobbler and even surprise Mama with a skillet of winter squash and greens, one of Carrie's favorites.

Supper went quickly. Carrie kept us enchanted with her window dressing escapades, including the one where the department head, lost in thought over her upcoming wedding, mistakenly put jeans and a tee shirt on a mannequin slated for an invitation only bash of the latest fashions imported directly from the runways of Paris, the gossip of her Brooklyn neighbors and the antics of Bloomingdale's most important Manhattan shoppers. Mama sent her to bed directly after dessert.

As Mama and I put the last dishes away Mama headed for her sewing machine to go over the patterns for baby clothes she had just purchased from the latest Sears catalogue. I went outdoors, drawn by the balmy weather and the gentle Indian summer breezes.

I put away the watering can and the gardening gloves left by the chrysanthemum bed in the rush to welcome Carrie. I looked up at the clear night sky, stars twinkling bright against an ebon background, and wondered which one had been responsible for sending Carrie back home.

Chapter Thirty-Four

C arrie's baby was born in early spring when the daisies, the bluebells and the buttercups were beginning to bloom in the meadows. He was as healthy as could be with a tuft of very dark hair and eyes as blue as the sky. Carrie and Jamie had decided to carry on Jamie's family line with the name Jameson Sloan Taylor, II.

Mama beamed as she first laid eyes on him, proud as could be. She was certain he was the spitting image of Papa.

Carrie and Jamie were intent upon calling him Tad, short for tadpole, since they both wanted to save him the distress of his coming second to his proud namesake, Jamie.

As for me, I couldn't stop looking at him, his perfect features, his little nose, and his large blue eyes. He looked perfect to spoil already, but I knew I couldn't let on my intentions.

Georgie, stationed at an army base just outside of Saigon where he was learning to be a medic, was delighted with the news of Tad's birth. He sent a set of small chopsticks to be used as pick-up sticks, a game of jacks, several tops carved out of a variety of woods, and a few balloons which he had purchased from a small shop in Saigon where he had gone on a weekend pass with his buddies to get to know the native Vietnamese. He included a very small teddy bear carved by one of his buddies from wood chipped from an old tree trunk not far from the base on a lonely night with only the moon and stars for light.

Carrie was agog with delight. She bathed Tad and fussed over him, decorating his nursery with the magical objects of childhood. Several mobiles hung from the ceiling, some with airplanes, some with teddy bears, and some with circus clowns. Pictures of Humpty Dumpty and Little Red Riding Hood decorated the walls of the small, old house she and Jamie had purchased on the only side street of Pottersville.

Jamie was busy turning an old, abandoned warehouse at the edge of town into a department store that would test the powers of the largest major stores in the business. He worked every daylight hour with the help of old Ethan Williams, a carpenter by trade but a plumber and electrician by hobby and a whiz at refurbishing old counters he rescued from the old five and dime he found in an old barn behind his house.

I helped Carrie as much as I could, bathing and feeding Tad, and walking him down the sidewalk when the weather was nice, especially past Beulah Walker's place so she could cluck over him and recite tips on bathing and feeding, the proper way to hold him, and how to avoid the perils of colic, spoiling, and diaper rash.

As we strolled the sidewalks of Pottersville the gentle spring breezes brought color to Carrie's cheeks and the bright morning sun brought warmth to Tad's buggy, a huge affair that Jamie had found in the pages of a Saks Fifth Avenue catalogue. As we rounded the corner to Main Street, Carrie turned quiet.

"A penny for your thoughts, Squirrel."

"I was just thinking how I miss the fashion world. The excitement, the shows, the unveiling of the latest designs. I would like to make Pottersville a destination like Paris and Milan.

"I have so many ideas for dresses and gowns, for skirts that are casual and can go anywhere, for fashion that can be dressed up or down, and for ball gowns that anyone can aspire to.

"When does Jamie's store open?"

"He's hoping it'll be ready by June. We've planned a grand opening that will have clowns and balloons, giveaways, games and contests. He has started hiring experts in millinery, shoes, and handmade jewelry as well as a few high-priced gems. I can hardly wait. I expect to be sketching by May. I'll be in charge of women's fashions."

"Sounds great. Who will be caring for Tad?"

"I'll be able to work at home a lot. But, when I'm at the store, I have great help in Jessie Larson who lives down the street and would love to watch Tad who she already adores. Her youngest, Daisy, is two and has already decided to adopt him as a playmate.

"Mama will fill in when she can. She has pulled a crib from the attic and has filled a dresser with blankets and baby clothes. She has knitted Tad several pairs of mittens even though winter is several months away."

Carrie paused, the scent of freshly sawn wood wafting in our direction. "Let's see how Jamie and Ethan are coming. I've packed them both a lunch."

As we neared the warehouse, once full of decay and overgrown with moss, the noise of buzz saws grew louder. The transformation was startling. The walls were built with beautiful Italian stone, the roof was imported grey slate, barn timbers gave a rustic look to the ceilings, and the large plate glass windows, roomy enough for mannequins to display the latest fashions, stood empty, the morning sunbeams playing upon the wide-planked oaken floors.

"Are you two ready for lunch?"

"We're famished. You've arrived just in time."

"Well, two such hard working men deserve a good lunch. I've packed coffee in a thermos, Mama's ham sandwiches, potato salad and slaw, and some strawberry pie."

Ethan put down his saw. "Perfect for an old bachelor like me."

Carrie set up lunch on a makeshift table and took Tad from his carriage. "I think we'll take a look around."

"Better be careful on the tour. The stairs need their risers and the hardwood hasn't arrived for the second floor."

Despite the half-finished building, Carrie could see a store bustling with customers, racks full of imports, and children begging to see the latest doll, teddy bear, and train collections. She had already designed the bags with the store's own color and seal.

When we returned, Carrie put the empty plates back into the hamper, Jamie and Ethan went back to work, and we strolled Main Street once again, the sun on our backs and Tad asleep in his carriage.

As we passed the village square, placed directly in the center of Main Street, the new statue of Ebenezer Potter, village founder, stood tall in the middle of a grassy rectangle, but now mired in controversy as a replacement sculpture for the first voted in just last week by the town council and deemed by Ebenezer's descendants, most of whom still lived in the village, to be far from a likeness of their venerated ancestor. A plaque to those from the village who had fought for their country in the wars since its founding stood in the corner. The opposite corner held bird feeders and beautiful gardens all carefully tended by the garden club.

As we greeted the few passers-by out for a morning stroll or shoppers bent on getting in for the latest sale at Hank Peterson's Dry Goods or dropping in for a coffee or a coke at Sandler's and rounded the corner to Carrie's street, greeting the elders now sitting on their porches to catch the afternoon sun, I mentally wished success for a department store built in a village most thought to be out in the middle of nowhere, backed only by the enthusiasm of youth.

Carrie put Tad in for his nap and I tidied up the parlor and the backyard, now strewn with toys. The daffodils and tulips, planted lovingly by the previous owners, were now in full bloom. I looked beyond the dilapidated and unused barn behind the property toward the horizon into which, despite its mist, I was certain I could see forever.

Chapter Thirty-Five

The opening of Taylor's department store came earlier than expected. Jason Pierce who owned a construction company in Mayberry finished an out-of-town job earlier than expected and came over to Pottersville to lend a hand to Jamie and Ethan. The sign over the front door spelled out "Taylor's" in large red cursive letters, a design created and constructed by a Syracuse sign company that shipped all over the world.

The weather was perfect and the crowds came in from all over, especially invited by Jamie and his folks, and by Carrie who enlisted the help of her former college mates and co-workers from Bloomingdales. A friend of Jamie's drove a limousine from the Syracuse airport and met people at the train station as well.

Mama and I spent time fussing over our outfits, ironing and primping, and adding the corsages Carrie insisted we wear. Alfonso Potter, the mailman who had taken over the route from Ken Walden who had retired after forty years of service, rang the bell, an armful of mail spilling out of his leather pouch. "I thought I'd come to the door today, Marylee, on such a special occasion. The whole town's buzzing."

"We're very proud of Carrie and Jamie. We want to make this day special for them."

"I think you've got a head start, Marylee. That number you're wearing ought to dazzle the daylights out of those out-of-towners."

"Why, thank you, Alfonso. I had it made by the best seamstress in all of Onondaga County, Sophie Archer, who spent a year in Italy learning how to sew as an apprentice to some of the greatest fashion designers in the world."

"I've got a special delivery from Georgie. You need to sign."

"He's never sent anything special delivery before. It must be something important.

"Thank you, Alfonso, and say 'hello' to Maddy."

"Will do. And, you two have the time of your lives. You both deserve it. The way you kept this farm going after Tyler went was a sight to behold. Have a cup of punch for me."

Mama fluffed up the skirt of the floral cotton she was wearing and fixed its flounce, the hem longer than usual in a bid to keep up with the newer fashions that would be hitting the stores this fall. She pulled out the straw hat Carrie had found her in Bloomie's, perfect for a hot summer day. She pinned on the orchid corsage Jamie's mother had sent, along with a note congratulating her and letting her know the orchid was the latest cross breed accepted into the poshest orchid society in the nation.

"I feel like a peacock."

"Mama, you look beautiful."

"If Papa could see me now he'd wonder what had become of me."

"He'd think you were the same beauty he married not long after he met you."

"Well, let's open John George's mail."

As Mama slit open the manila envelope a letter and several photographs slipped out of the packet. Mama laid them out in a line and opened the letter.

"Dear Mama, Carrie and Annie May,

I miss you all more than I can say. This place is lonely and the climate is very humid with hills covered with dense forests. I cannot wait until I can be home again.

I have sent you some photographs of the city of Saigon which a buddy of mine took on a weekend pass when we toured the city. I have also sent a picture of Anh Ly, a girl I met in Saigon at a USO dance. She is kind and shy and her smile lights up the room. We were married this weekend because I have heard several rumors that our unit will soon be sent to the front.

I plan to bring Anh Ly home as soon as I am mustered out. She very much wants to come to America and can't wait to meet you.

I can't write much more because it will soon be lights out. But, I hope the farm is thriving and harvest time will reap the biggest crops ever.

I love you all and hope the best fortunes will shine on all of you. I can't wait to see you.

> Your loving son and brother,
> John George

Mama took a deep breath, then spoke. "We must be happy for John George. He's so far away from home. "He's so young for marrying. But, Papa and I were that age when we eloped against both our parents' wishes.

"I will send Anh Ly a ring I've kept for safekeeping handed down from Granny's kin and a length of homespun turned out from Alma Peterson's loom.

"Now, we must get to Carrie's. That store, with all its newfangled do-dads, must be hopping by now. Why they are even getting in some elves that turn and do a dance for the Christmas windows."

As Mama and I drove into Pottersville, the windows of the truck wide open to let the summer air in, Mama hanging onto her hat despite the pearl tipped hat pin Carrie had included with the hat box she had shipped from New York, I thought of Georgie getting married in such a strange place.

I had lost Carrie to Jamie and now I had lost Georgie to a girl from a far-away land I didn't even know. Despite the excitement of the grand opening loneliness was setting in.

I decided to put on a good face for Mama's sake. After all, her pride in Carrie was plain to see.

I followed the parade that was marching down Main Street, heralding the grand opening of Taylor's department store. I parked in a field behind the former abandoned warehouse and helped Mama out, her new shoes pinching a bit and the skirt of her new dress threatening to blow with the wind.

The squirrels in the field were dashing off to the side and the crowds had trampled the daisies. But, the wild vetch and the lupines and asters had survived.

The sun was beaming down from a cloudless sky and birds, sent from their perches by the noise of the crowds were chirping everywhere and looking for a place to roost.

As we walked toward the refurbished structure finished in sandstone, the elegance of urban chic contrasting with unplanned rural sprawl, a large red banner announcing the grand opening draped above the plate glass doors of the entrance, their sleek, modern lines softened by a scrolled mahogany framing, I hoped only that my mint green linen topped by a beige summer jacket would stay uncreased until the festivities were over.

Chapter Thirty-Six

The summer after my first year as a full-time teacher at Baldwinsville High was a balmy and humid one. Nevertheless, the wild roses and geraniums bloomed in the meadows and the wild lilies were more spectacular than ever. Uncle John, used to all kinds of weather, still sprayed, cultivated and fertilized, despite the pesky flies and mosquitoes that came out on the wettest days.

Taylor's department store was thriving and Carrie was expecting a baby in fall. Tad was thrilled and was helping to decorate the nursery while Mama was filling drawers with infant overalls, baby bonnets, and fancy crocheted sweaters.

Jeb, who had visited from time to time, was taking a week off to stay and soak up the farm life. Will, who had returned from research in New York to set up a veterinary practice, had volunteered to take him on a working tour the moment he arrived, letting him off on his own to try his hand at cultivating and fertilizing the cabbages and beans, the squash and the pumpkins, all county fair winners gleaned from Georgie's cross-breeding, and the many fields of feed corn Uncle John had turned to for cash crop.

Jeb arrived, tanned and fit after a Hawaii vacation with Martha and Peter and his latest conquest. "How's the new teacher?"

"Had a great year. How about you?"

"Company's doing fine. We're turning a profit and expanding with an added facility overseas. Dad's beside himself with joy. The company that destroyed him with the unethical takeover is sinking fast. They can't keep up with the competition.

"We've been able to attract the best and the brightest. They're vying to be with us. We've got the most modern facilities in the business and we've put in a great work ethic. All the Ph.Ds. get a month off to study in a vacation spot anywhere in the world. We've had requests for climates as sunny as Mexico and Brazil, and as wet as the Amazon rainforests. They've really come through for us. We've got patents galore for a company so short a time in business."

"I'm so glad for you, Jeb. You deserve it. You've put in a lot of hours chasing across continents to catch the latest research first-hand. It looks like it has paid off.

"And I'm glad for your dad too. He had a lot of faith in you.

"Now, let's go see Mama. She's been waiting to feed you and put a little meat on you because she is certain city folk don't eat right."

Mama, smitten by Jeb's good humor and sunny disposition early on, went right to the stove to stir the pot roast gravy, dish up the mashed potatoes, and set out her green bean casserole fresh from the oven all perfectly browned and crisped.

"Mrs. Parker, you look wonderful. It must be all those hours in the sun tending those beautiful gardens which have bloomed like a magazine picture."

"Now, Jeb, you stop flattering me and eat. You're a little too thin this visit."

"It must be that I haven't had time to check in on you and Annie May this year too often. New York and Paris chefs don't know a thing about down home cooking."

"Well, it looks like you forget to eat while you're flitting all over Europe. Now, you sit down and dig in.

"How are your parents? They must have a time keeping track of you."

"They're fine. And, of course, my mother wants me

to settle down as usual. But, I'm way too busy for that. Someday I might surprise her if I find someone who is half the girl Annie May is."

"You eat up and we'll put some meat on you for all those trips to Europe. I have a fresh baked cherry pie cooling on the sill and some fresh made ice cream from Stuarts' dairy down the road."

Jeb sent Mama to the parlor while we did the dishes and scrubbed the pots, making sure every last one was in its proper place. Jeb looked fine with a dish towel in his hand.

"And, what is that vehicle you have parked in the driveway?"

"That's an MG roadster, conservative enough to satisfy the old guard and exciting enough to catch the risk takers. It's a bid to look successful in a competitive market. And, I got it in a swap directly from London so no cash outlay.

"Maybe we'll take a spin when I'm done in by farm work."

"I'll come prepared. It doesn't look as slow as Mama's trusty old truck."

"I think I'll turn in. It's been a long drive."

"See you very early in the morning. Farm days are half over before Manhattan is out of bed."

"Will do. Dream of a rosy future."

Will was at the farm at four a.m. ready to roll Jeb out of bed but Jeb was dressed and ready with boots and coveralls and a hat he had purchased at an Agway on the road two towns over. Uncle John was happy to have Will back, even though it was for only a week.

Will and Jeb hit it off right away. The week went fast, Jeb's muscles ached, but he was even tanner and more fit than when he had arrived. He left just like he came, on the road at eight in the morning with a package of Mama's best cookies and a ham and cheese to stave off his hunger until he arrived back in Brooklyn.

As I watched Jeb's car disappear into the horizon, clouds of dust in its wake, I thought of Georgie, so far from home in a land of relentless heat and densely forested mountains. I must remember to pack up some photos of the cabbages and squash almost ready for early harvest and include some of Mama's oatmeal raisin cookies and a few trinkets for Anh Ly.

With the sun hard upon my back the warmth of summer was in the air. I picked up my pace and hurried back into the kitchen. Mama would need help cleaning up the pile of dishes from the pancakes and slab bacon breakfast she served in a last ditch effort to fill out Jeb's lanky frame.

Chapter Thirty-Seven

It was a gray day when two uniformed officers from the Syracuse armory arrived to give us the news that Georgie had been killed by an enemy sniper as he was carrying the wounded to safety. The officers left with us some letters written by Georgie's buddies praising his courage and the little kindnesses he was known for among his comrades.

Mama was inconsolable and I had an empty place in my heart where Georgie had always been. The two officers from the armory presented Mama with an American flag and Pastor Brown gave a eulogy as we laid Georgie to rest in the small family graveyard up on the far hill next to Papa.

Aunt Maybelle drove from Lancaster County to be with Mama and Josie, who had become very fond of Georgie, came in from Washington where she and Max had been married at City Hall and Max had begun a job with the State Department. Will popped in as often as he could to provide a male presence.

Carrie was beside herself and lent a hand whenever

she could. She peeled potatoes and made endless casseroles so Mama wouldn't have to cook.

"Josie, you look radiant. Marriage seems to agree with you."

"As much as I've seen of it. It was a whirlwind marriage so Max could take a job he so much wanted. But, we promised our folks a more formal wedding in Iowa and posh reception in New York so until then we are vagabonds.

"Max is the perfect husband. He cooks and keeps the cars running while I head for the couch after a day of job searching."

"You sound like the ideal couple. You better watch out that a D.C. magazine doesn't run a story on you before you've had a chance to settle down.

You should be ready to be snapped up by the farming industry while you're there. I hear you designed a whole new thresher while you were in Boston."

"I did. But, the patent belongs to Middleton's in Boston so they'll be manufacturing it and I won't see it until it's on somebody's farm."

"Well, you'll know you've made a contribution to modernizing farming."

"My father will think it'll get in the way of real farming. He loathes modern equipment.

"I checked with The Smithsonian to see if there were jobs in the farm equipment exhibit but they told me to come back in six weeks. And, Max doesn't know where he'll be assigned when he finishes training. I think I'm a girl without a job."

"Things will look up when you're settled and Max has a firm assignment. Until then, I'm going to enlist your help for a skillet of fried potatoes Iowa style for supper."

"Will do. And, I think I'll get those clothes out of the washer and through the ringer so I can get them out on the clothes line before dark."

"Josie, you've been such a help. I don't know what I would have done without you this week."

"I think you would have done just fine. But, Georgie was like a little brother to me. When Kenny left home there was such a gap but Georgie helped fill it.

"And, his joy in farming was catching. His face lit up at the sight of a new spring seed catalogue."

"Georgie's life was in those fields. I never remember a day when he wasn't on Papa's lap at planting time, barely able to talk yet, and begging to drive the tractor.

"I'm going in to start supper. Mama has barely eaten in the last few days. I'm going to see if your skillet potatoes will tempt her. I'll get a start on the pot roast."

As I spoke Will came through the door with a load of onions he received in payment from a new family in town for reviving their pet goat who had eaten some fertilizer from an open sack lying around in an old barn behind their house. "How about some fresh dug onions?

"Is there anything a male can lend a hand at around here that needs doing? I see your Uncle John has already left."

"He left early to take Aunt Mabel to the Mayberry Chamber of Commerce pancake supper. The garden club has planted a new bulb garden at the post office and tended the gardens around the Mayberry town hall for ten years. Aunt Mabel is accepting the award.

"You can put the tractor back in the barn. The transmission quit and Uncle John didn't have time to tinker. How's the new vet?"

"Busy. Between fixing up the cats and dogs of the village, I've been trying to stop the equine flu that has hit the horse population and the flu that's sweeping through the cattle stock. I need to call a meeting for better and cleaner conditions for disease control. Most of the dairy and horse farms have been using the same methods for generations."

"I know they'll listen to you. They haven't had a good vet around here in years. It's been hard for the locals to wait for nearby city vets to ride the circuit when disease was leveling their stock."

"My folks send their condolences and will lend a hand at any time you need it. I know Jester misses Georgie like I do. Ma's planning to send some casseroles over to lighten your cooking load for next week."

"Thanks, Will. Georgie was so fond of your folks."

As Will left and Josie hung the wash in the lovely, summer air I started the pot roast, making sure to add our best onions, carrots, and the fresh parsley I picked from the garden just outside the barn. I would let it simmer until I pulled the dry clothes off the line, letting its aroma drift out onto the summer breezes now gently tugging at wet shirt sleeves and the hems of light cotton skirts, the leaves of the nearby maple swaying softly to its rhythm.

Supper went fast with Mama capable of speaking

only a few amenities. Josie and I cleaned up as early as we could.

Georgie's spirit was everywhere, in the moonlit fields, and in the wild rose he laid on my bed when Ollie Webster broke my lovelorn fifth grade heart. But, I was determined to put my tears aside and keep my promise to Georgie to tend to Mama.

As I lay in bed, I looked out the open windows into the dark. I remembered how I ran into Georgie's room when a shooting star streaked across the sky in hopes he could see it too. The night sky was lit up with what seemed to be hundreds of stars but only one was twinkling. I was certain it was Georgie's soul looking down on us.

Chapter Thirty-Eight

Fall brought cold, brisk winds and the signs of an early winter. The reds, the rusts, the oranges and yellows of the leaves of maples, hawthorns and elms lay across lawns and sidewalks and walkways, wafting along with a gentle wind and playfully settling and crunching beneath the feet of even the most careful walkers. The sun beat down upon the mums and the asters, bathing them in warmth and drying up the mists and dews of the early morning.

I went back to Baldwinsville Central with a heavy heart but with an urge to enlighten every student who sat in front of me. Richard called me often to fill in for his freshman classes while he was away or working furiously on deadline to finish his first manuscript.

Taylor's department store was basking in the glory of weekend events, clowns and pony rides, fashion shows and horseshoe contests, which drew large crowds and counted it a huge success by its first annual founding day celebration bash. Carrie's lines of casual clothing and ball gowns were selling out at a rapid pace both at Taylor's and at Bloomie's, where both Carrie and Jamie had kept their previous contacts, and were poised to compete in the fashion scene of both Paris and Milan.

Carrie's baby arrived on a sunny, autumn day, with birth hair the color of Carrie's and a lusty squall that announced her early arrival. Carrie and Jamie named her Alice Rose, the namesake of two of their favorite grandmothers, but both called her Allie.

Tad was smitten with Allie and followed Carrie and Jessie Larson, who had come in to help, around with rattles and teddy bears, bath towels and rubber ducks, and the stray dachshund puppy they had taken in named Oscar after one of Carrie's favorite designers.

Mama still spoke very little and the twinkle that lit up the soft blue of her eyes ever since I could remember was gone. But, she was cooking as often as she could and caring for Tad and Allie when her spirits allowed.

Pastor Brown stopped in for weekly visits and Will came for supper if he had a free evening. Uncle John checked on Mama every morning. "Marylee, the hired hands miss your oatmeal raisin cookies and your ham and pot roast lunches."

It was a rare warm and sunny evening when Will

breezed in for a Friday night supper, a basket of apples in one hand and a jug of cider in the other. "Fresh picked from the orchard behind the animal hospital. Cider hand-pressed by the Coopers across the street."

"Sounds like a rare treat. You can roll up your sleeves and help me get this chicken in the roaster."

"Will do. How's Baldwinsville?"

"I've got a great class. We're on to the classics already. How's the vet business?"

"I've been saving for a research lab in the back of the animal hospital and I've got it almost set up. The lab in New York where I spent the summer has been very generous with their cast-offs. I've been keeping up with the latest research on equine flu and I can't wait to set up a study. There are those in the field who think there is a crossover to human disease as well."

"Sounds interesting. I think you're heading for the Nobel prize."

"I would like to cure all the ills on the planet. But, I guess one step at a time will do."

I set the table and called Mama into the kitchen. As we sat, the roast chicken steaming on its platter, the mashed potatoes and yellow squash casserole nearby, Mama handed me an unopened envelope she had pulled from the morning mail, its stamp postmarked Vietnam, its address The Parker Family, its return address unknown. I opened it and read aloud.

Dear Parker Family,

I am a friend of Anh Ly. My name is Chi Linh. We have lived on the streets of Saigon together since our small village was ransacked and destroyed by the war. Our families were unable to feed us so we made our way to the city to beg for food, taking shelter wherever we could.

I was present at Anh Ly's marriage to John George and we celebrated through the night and it was a joyous occasion. But, after he returned to his army base Anh Ly was unable to contact him again as the war got worse to the north to tell him she was to have a baby.

Anh Ly's baby was born in an alleyway in Saigon. She was a beautiful baby and Anh Ly named her Mai Li. When she could no longer feed her she begged her family to give her baby refuge and returned to the streets of Saigon where she lost her life to starvation and disease.

Anh Ly made me promise if anything happened to her that I would send news of the baby to you and the only photograph she possessed of Mai Li which I have enclosed in this humble letter.

I have been unable to find news of Mai Li's welfare and am uncertain if she still resides with the family of Anh Ly because they are very poor.

Anh Ly loved John George very much and prayed every day for his safety.

I have included the address of a small tavern where they sometimes give me work and where I can be reached if you need me.

I send my best regards to you and all your family.

> Sincerely.
> Chi Linh
> Devoted Friend of Anh Ly

We stared at the photograph, a small, thin child with the almond eyes and straight black hair of Anh Ly and the remaining features the spitting image of Georgie.

Will dried the dishes and left for home, weary from a day at his beloved animal clinic and Mama went upstairs. I tidied up alone with my thoughts.

I thought about our ancestors, their hardships, their deeds, their courage and their fears, their tales wrapped in a stack of journals in the heat of an attic above, their spirits so often about the house. I climbed the stairs to my room, avoiding the creaky treads, weariness overtaking me as I tiptoed down the old, narrow hallway, its faded tan carpet threadbare from years of use.

As I prepared for bed, I thought of the child Mai Li alone in a country so far away. I prayed for her safety as I turned down the heart and daisy chain quilt I had entered into the county fair so long ago. As I lay in bed I stared at the night sky and searched for the star that shone the brightest hoping it would shine over Mai Li one day as well.

Chapter Thirty-Nine

I packed my bags as the first snows of winter began to fall. I had taken leave of Baldwinsville Central to search for the child Mai Li and Max had pulled a number of strings to hasten the passport process.

Will had refused to let me go alone, insisting he had loved Georgie too, and closed down the vet hospital until we returned, leaving a young student on call.

I had extracted a promise from Carrie that she would look after Mama, no matter how busy she was. She took leave from Taylor's and hired Jessie Larson to care for Tad and Allie, bringing them for supper to brighten Mama's day.

Max had arranged for military transport and the trip was uneventful but we were on our own in Saigon. We were directed to lodgings in a fairly rundown former inn on a side street of the city and worked to formulate a plan as we unpacked.

The owner of the inn found us a local who agreed to take us to Anh Ly's family's village. The heat and the humidity were overwhelming but the local, Minh

Dong, a former farmer who had migrated to Saigon when his own village had been devastated, was able to secure a fairly reliable vehicle, a second hand French Renault that sputtered only occasionally.

Minh Dong, who had not been able to find employment since he had arrived in Saigon but lived with his wife's family who were all employed by the government, explained that we had arrived at the end of the wet season so we wouldn't be deluged with downpours, but we would run into some very old roads that had never been repaired since the war.

The village we arrived at was filled with dilapidated bamboo structures, set about almost randomly. We asked at every home we could find the living quarters of Anh Ly's family and were directed to a small, run down house at the edge of the village. An old man, with few teeth, answered the door to Minh Dong's timid knock. As he heard our request, he called a younger woman to the door.

"Hello. I am Cam Nhu, cousin to Anh Ly. I the only one here to speak English. How do I help you?"

"We would like to find out about Anh Ly's baby Mai Li. I am the sister of her husband John George

Parker, an American. We had word from a friend of Anh Ly's that she had left her baby here."

"We took her baby in but not able to keep her. We have many mouths to feed and we struggle with no food since village was destroyed. We have seen many starve. We left village when it was attacked but returned when we thought it safe. All our fields destroyed and nowhere to get food. Some have gone to the city to beg but the rest scratch about for food.

"We are fourteen in our shelter of one room. Mai Li cry a lot because we have no food to give her. Babies gotten by Americans not looked upon well by some people because they blame the war for their misery.

"We had so much hunger when Mai Li here. A man came and offer us money enough to feed us all for a year if we give Mai Li to him. We have no choice. Her sacrifice has kept us from starving."

"Who was this man?"

"He work for a place called Pleasure Palace. It is in Saigon."

We said our goodbyes to Cam Nhu and thanked her for the information. We left with our wishes for a speedy end to the war that was ravishing the countryside.

As we rode back to the inn, Minh Dong at the wheel coaxing the Renault along the roads torn up by jeeps and tanks and fleeing vehicles, we sat silent, oblivious of the countryside, flat and grassy, stretching for miles, some of it along swollen and murky waterways.

We enlisted Minh Dong's help in finding a café for an evening meal and he suggested a place he thought we might find news of what we were looking for. "93-95 Tu Do Street, Café and Bar Imperial. Popular spot with GI's and underworld black market. Crooks mingle looking for unsuspecting Americans to fleece. Pose like innocent American and maybe you get news of Pleasure Palace."

Café and Bar Imperial, a French open-air bar with tiled floors, zinc counters, tables open to both streets, and waiters with white shirts dressed smartly in khakis and flip-flops, was hopping when we arrived, let off by Minh Dong who cautioned us that he would return in exactly two hours.

Will approached the bar while I found a table, close by the street, and sat, the evening a little cooler than the day but still with the heavy humidity we had found since we had arrived in Saigon. I waited for Will to return to order.

We ordered beef strips, a plate of dumplings, and a large bowl of spicy noodle soup. Will had two glasses of champagne in his hands he had brought from the bar.

"The bartender says a man who owns the Pleasure Palace frequents this place every night since he's been tending bar here. He is looking for rich Americans or wealthy Arab sheiks or those who represent them as clients. He has many repeat customers and considers his wares the best in the business.

"The bartender said if I'm interested I should make myself known to him. He was pointed out as that man sitting two tables down with a mustache, dark hair, and a rather sinister look. I think I'll approach him after we order dessert."

"You better be careful. The men around him look as sinister as he is."

"I plan to exercise some caution. And, I think I see some strong arms hovering about who look like they are protecting the interests of this bar and café."

Will rose from our table as soon as dessert was served, an apple tart of sorts, and threaded his way to the man two tables over. The man looked up, a shifty look on his face, and questioned Will. The conversation, despite the smoky atmosphere and the constant chatter, drifted over.

"American?"

"Yes."

"What do you want?" A thick French accent accompanied his words.

"I represent an Arab emir who wants to stay anonymous.

"He might be interested in what you have to offer. He has requested that I look over your stock and make a judgment."

"How many."

"He might be interested in ten or fifteen, depending on how good your stock is."

The man scowled. "I have the best in the business. I demand unmarked cash paid all at once upfront. If there is any double-crossing, your Arab emir won't see his next birthday."

"I understand. When can I look them over?"

"Tomorrow. I write the directions on this napkin. There is an old woman who lives there and watches the place. She will answer the door. Tell her Hugo sent you."

Will returned to our table and whispered. "I will

pay the bartender for our meal and go to the rest rooms. Minh Dong is outside. You walk slowly out of the café and get into Minh Dong's car. I will leave by the back door and I will meet you on the next block behind the café."

It was here that my fright took over but I worked hard to hide it from Will. A few minutes after Will left I slipped slowly out of the café and into Minh Dong's waiting car. I gave him the directions and he headed for the next block, slowly so we did not arouse suspicion.

Back at the hotel we formulated our plans for tomorrow. Minh Dong would pick us up at nine. We would get to the Pleasure Palace about ten. Minh Dong and I would wait on the next street over while Will entered the building.

Will would present himself at the Pleasure Palace and explain that he was there on behalf of a wealthy emir. If all went well, Will would ask to see the girls in a separate room and see them each alone so he could choose. He would pick a few before he picked Mai Li who he was counting on recognizing from the tattered photograph Chi Linh had sent.

Will packed a pillow in a duffel bag and poked

some holes in the bottom. He also packed a needle filled with a tranquilizer that would put the child out until we were safely away. When he had gotten Mai Li alone he would gently tranquilize her, remove the pillow from the duffel, place Mai Li inside, and leave the house from the entrance that seemed the safest at the time and meet us the next block over.

The plan was risky, but from what we heard by asking around, none of the black market rings were ever bothered because they regularly paid off the police.

I went to sleep that night, not certain that I would get much rest in a strange bed so far away from home but I hoped only for Will's safety and the safety of Mai Li. I put the shade on the small window down because there was nothing to see but buildings with bright shining lights blocking the night sky and the moon.

Chapter Forty

The sun poured into the room as I rose to get ready for the day's events. I could also hear a stirring of activity in the room next door which was Will's.

I decided to pick from the few clothes I brought something fairly bland because I didn't want to stand out either at the inn or on the street. Duc Quan, the inn owner, jovial despite the hardships of the war, set out an American breakfast that made us wish for home.

Minh Dong arrived on time and we set out, Will carefully guarding his duffel, which many GI's about the streets of Saigon were carrying, so it wouldn't look out of place. The heat was oppressive and the dry season very humid.

We all said nothing, the tension filling the car. Will spoke. "It's okay, Annie May, we'll make it. But, if I'm not out by twelve call the American Embassy and get help."

"I have the number of the direct contact Max gave me. The embassy contact has been briefed on our mission here.

"The diplomatic corps isn't too happy about our goal but they promised to keep it under wraps. If anything happens they have promised us security and an offense to come to our aid if we need it."

"Let's hope nothing goes wrong. We don't want to chance the lines of communication getting all fouled up. Just keep your eye on the time."

"I will. And, Will, you be very careful."

"I will. I know how much this means to us."

The rest of the drive was in silence, Minh Dong watching the traffic which seemed to be teeming this time of day, thinning out as we took the side streets to get to the Pleasure Palace, hidden away in one of the poorest sections of Saigon. The neighbors, nowhere to be seen, apparently living behind closed doors and oblivious of the dealings of the Pleasure Palace, most likely paid off by Hugo and his mob.

We let Will off on the next block over and waited. As Will disappeared around the corner my fear level rose but I decided to appear calm for Minh Dong's sake. "How long have you been in Saigon?"

"Many months. Our village destroyed by war and we must come to my wife's family. Lucky for us they have good jobs with the government and they take us in. We have seven mouths to feed.

"We lose house and rice paddies. Not safe."

"Are there schools for your children?"

"In Saigon there not enough schools or teachers for children. My wife teach them to read and write in Vietnamese but she not know French. Her sisters in her household know French but too busy with government jobs to teach.

"At home in our small village we have enough food. We have big rice paddy, a water buffalo, and sell enough crop to get tea and fish.

"I get jobs driving tourist sometime but not enough. I leave my name with every hotel and inn in Saigon. No jobs for farmers in Saigon."

As the time began to drag and Minh Dong could sense my fear we turned to other subjects. Minh Dong told me of the tales handed down by his people and the folk music from centuries ago he seemed to love. "When rice paddies flood we have puppet show on water. Men stand in water and hide behind screen. Move puppets beneath the water. Puppets dance and sing on water. All villagers come to celebrate the harvest."

As we spoke, Will finally appeared from around the corner heading directly for our car. Minh Dong turned on the motor and Will, looking both tense and flustered and relieved at the same time jumped in.

"Go. We'd better get out of here. Head for the airport and make it as fast as you can but drive slowly around the corner. We don't need to arouse suspicion."

Will turned to me. "We did it. We have Mai Li. If all goes right she'll awake when we're in the air."

I wasn't certain who to silently thank but I decided to keep my composure. "Did you arouse any suspicion?"

"I don't think so. The old lady who watches them during the day seems harmless. She naps most of the time. They're kept there by fear."

"Did you have any trouble getting Mai Li?"

"Not really. She was frightened at first, but I was able to tranquilize her almost right away. The others stayed where they were and asked no questions. They're half-starved and live in extreme fear."

"I wired Max last night from the inn in the code we agreed on back home. There should be a plane gassed up and ready to leave as soon as we reach the airport."

I fought sleep in order to remain alert and coaxed Minh Dong to go as fast as he could. "How much farther?"

"Not much. I go as fast as I can. We don't want to be stopped."

"You've done us a great service, Minh Dong. We are very grateful."

"American soldier babies not wanted here. You are different. You give good care."

As we rounded the next corner, the airport loomed in front. Minh Dong drove across the field to a small building that appeared to be US military. I rolled down the window of the Renault to speak to the officer who stepped out in front of us. "We have permission to board a plane. Code word "Maxwell Oliver.""

The officer waved us to a small plane sitting near the runway, its propeller going and its door opened. "Have a safe trip."

"Thanks for the help."

Minh Dong raced across the bumpy field to pull alongside the plane. "You go fast."

I hugged Minh Dong and promised to write. Will pressed a wad of bills in his hand. "For your family."

We raced to the door of the plane, Will holding the

duffel in his arms. The pilot helped us aboard and slammed the door shut.

The plane took us farther and farther into the clouds and into our own thoughts. We stopped to refuel twice, making sure Mai Li ate if we could entice her.

We arrived home, Josie, who had taken a crash course in French to travel with Max, awaiting us to explain to Mai Li whose only language was French, her whereabouts. Mama and Carrie stood by.

Mai Li was afraid to sleep so Carrie stayed with her, singing her the only lullaby she knew. Will left and I slipped between the sheets of my bed without turning the coverlet down. I was certain the night was full of stars, bright ones, twinkling ones, and those that streaked across the darkened sky. But, tonight they would have to sparkle without me.

Chapter Forty-One

I t was a beautiful, sunny day on Strawberry Hill when Will proposed. The berries were plump and ripe, and the buttercup, wild rose, and lavender asters were rife among them.

It was not a formal proposal because despite Will becoming the most sought after animal doctor in Onondaga County he was still as shy as the day I met him.

"Annie May, would you consider settling down with me and raising a small brood of Vanderworts?"

I was tongue tied. I was certain that at least one of those fancy women he met in New York would have gotten him long ago. "I never thought you'd think I was suitable as the wife of a famous scientist, too skinny to fill out a ball gown, all thumbs at getting gussied up."

"I fell for you when I met you at thirteen, all freckles and the gawkiest girl I had ever seen, ready to beat every boy in arm wrestling or chasing after a horse before it had strayed too far.

"But, I was always afraid you'd turn me down. You

were the most independent girl I ever met and the most responsible. I never thought you'd have me."

I stared at Will, the handsomest boy I had ever seen, including Charlie Jasper who was voted king of both the junior and the senior class. Somehow it seemed like we had always been together without our knowing.

"I would be proud to be your wife."

As we stood, two people on the top of a hill we knew so well, it seemed like the universe was in perfect harmony, the moon to replace the sun which was setting in a wide swath of beautiful pastel colors, the sky to soon host a multitude of shining stars.

Will held me as we walked back through the meadows as tightly as he had ever held me when he kept me from falling into an ice pond in the midst of a stormy winter or from the path of a runaway horse. The sweet scent of the phlox, the trillium, and the blue chicory rose up about us.

Mai Li had been with us eight months now and had filled out with Mama's cooking but she was still silent, robbed of her words and her trust since the early years of her infancy. But, Doc Anderson assured us she would speak when she was ready.

Tad took an interest in her whereabouts and she adored Allie. Oscar was her constant companion when she could find him.

We had set aside a room for Mai Li and Carrie had filled it with the handmade quilts Taylor's department store carried and the ruffled curtains and soft pink dresser top doilies she pressed the sewing room to create. She filled it with dolls of all kinds and Mai Li found her favorite, a doll she named Emma who she carried with her at all times.

Will left for home and I went inside to find Carrie preparing supper, Tad insisting he should help, and Allie asleep in the crib upstairs. I pulled out a peeler and began to search for some onions and some peppers to mix up a potato casserole.

As we sat around the table, Mama offering Mai Li tidbits of the ham Carrie had baked and the cherries and pineapple that covered it, I made my announcement.

"Will and I are planning to tie the knot. We'd like a summer wedding."

Carrie gushed her surprise and her happiness. "Why Will has been underfoot all these years. I never would have guessed, Annie May. Jamie will be so

327

surprised and happy for you. He thinks the world of Will."

"That's short notice, Anabel May. We have to notify the kinfolk and get Pastor Brown."

"I know, Mama, but Will and I will do all the work."

As Carrie and I cleaned up and Tad kept us company bringing the dishes from the table one by one Carrie could talk of nothing else but the wedding. "Annie May, you can have any dress Taylor's has in stock or we can design one. And, as for the invitations Elvira Dunkin in hats does calligraphy. And, you can pick out anything in the store for something new."

I hugged Carrie and put the dried dishes away. As Carrie and the children said their goodbyes I hurried up to bed, weary from the day but unable to sleep. I wondered if Will was unable to sleep as well.

The wedding was held on Strawberry Hill on what I thought was the most beautiful day of the year. The comforting warmth of the sun beat down upon us and the late summer wild orchids, asters, and anemone were in full bloom.

Carrie was matron of honor and Jeb, who had taken an interest in Will's fledgling research lab, had flown in to be best man. Mai Li, who was looking ever so much like Georgie, was flower girl in a beautiful pink dress Carrie had designed feeling very much like a princess. Tad was ring bearer and took his role seriously, asking Carrie every five minutes whether the rings were placed right on the tiny pillow.

I felt very much a part of the Earth and its universe as I stood reciting my vows, the soft afternoon breezes ruffling the skirts of my white cotton dress, a string of late summer wild orchids running through the French twist in my hair.

I had picked my white daisy bouquet from the meadow behind the barn and fastened it with silk and grosgrain ribbon the colors of a misty rainbow after a spring rain. I had added the daisy I had dried and kept that Will had plucked for my hair so many years ago on a silly trip through the meadow to peek at the eggs of a late spring robin's nest stuck under the rafters of the barn.

We celebrated all afternoon and far into the night. Square dancing in a moonlit barn, roasted marshmallows and old familiar tunes sung around an open fire, and tables of tiny little sandwiches, salads and slaws, and pies and cakes trailed in from as far away as Texas.

Mama was as proud as could be and introduced Will's folks to all her kinfolk. Will's Ma brought a Dutch butter cake, pans of pastries, and the mild and creamy cheeses of her homeland.

I was certain the spirits of our ancestors were celebrating with us. A half-Indian maiden dancing wildly under the moon, a gypsy woman swirling her skirts to the haunting music of the gypsy soul.

We said goodbye to Mama and Carrie and headed for New York, a three-day honeymoon where Jeb was waiting to show us the sights and Will was waiting to connect to as many high-powered research labs as he could.

We drove all night beneath a full moon, the trees silvery in the moonlight. I barely noticed the stars as I thought about our future. The towns we passed through looked all the same in their silence, their churches and schools dark, their shops closed for the night, the windows of their homes all shuttered. I decided to recite every silly poem I knew to keep us awake until we reached New York.

Chapter Forty-Two

Will rose before dawn and before the dew had a chance to settle on the meadow grasses and the seedlings newly sprouted in the fields. He was anxious to pore over his slides and his microscopes before the meal of the day began.

We had decided to stay with Mama to help run the farm since Uncle John was spending most of his time nursing his lumbago and to do the chores Mama could no longer do. Will had set up a building behind the barn and with the help of Jeb had stocked it with the latest up-to-date lab equipment that science catalogues had to offer.

I rose as well and went out to check the chicken coop which we had added for Mai Li. The hens were good layers and it was many a day that Mai Li had nearly enough eggs to make a dozen.

I shaded my eyes as the sun came up and thought of Georgie as I surveyed the fields. The seedlings were growing tall and strong and many were the cross-breeds he had spent so long perfecting.

The sun rose, its hues of orange and yellow mixed with a touch of pink less brilliant than the sunset, softly breaking through the dark to bring on the day. I headed back to the kitchen to start breakfast.

Taylor's was closed for renovations and Jamie was coming with Carrie and the children. I was anxious to get a head start on the pancake batter and fry up the sausages.

As I pushed open the screen door, I heard a commotion in the driveway. Jamie's new truck, his pride and joy, was stuck and Tad and Allie were both insisting to carry the breakfast casserole Carrie had made from a recipe she had gotten from the New York chef who had come in to give a demonstration in Taylor's cookery department. Carrie made the decision to carry the casserole herself and give them each one of their toys to carry. "It's a beautiful spring day. Is there anything I can do?"

"Just sit and look beautiful. I'm sure you can use it."

"Thanks, Annie May. How's the new bride?"

"Hardly a bride. It's been a year and a half. Will and I are expecting in June."

"Did Doc Anderson give you the go-ahead to keep working?"

"He said everything's fine. I can work as long as I want. But, Baldwinsville isn't certain. They would like me to leave before the end of the year. I'm looking around for a substitute.

"It will give me time to be more of a help to Will in the lab before the baby comes. Now, let's get down to business and put that casserole in the oven to warm.

"Who wants to go and get Uncle Will?"

"I do."

"Me too."

"Well, you take Oscar and round up Mai Li and then you can all go out."

Will allowed himself to be dragged from the makeshift building, his hair tousled from a pretend wrestling match, Mai Li on his shoulders, a ball in his hand to toss for Oscar, and Tad and Allie pulling on his shirtsleeves begging for their turn.

We sat around the table, Jamie washed up from his grease-filled bout with his new truck, Mama's knitting laying on a parlor table, Oscar poised to pounce on dropped crumbs, and Mai Li nestled against Mama's shoulder.

Carrie dished out the casserole and I found a platter for the sausages.

"Hey, Will, how's the mad scientist?"

"Great. Got a new shipment of test tubes and slides and my microscopes are top of the line. I'm ready to set up a study when I can get a few minutes away from patching up the critters. Need help with that new monster of yours?"

"I could use it. Straight from the factory and it sputters and conks out."

"We'll get it purring. How's the shopkeeper?"

"Up and running. We've got bids from three new towns to move in and set up shop. We've hit pay dirt with Carrie's new line of modest clothing. We can't keep them on the racks. And, her ball gowns have hit the Paris workrooms with our exclusive label. We've put in a runway and are setting up a fashion show for August. Even Bloomie's buyers will be there."

As Jamie spoke, he looked at Carrie and it was plain to see, despite his many absences on business, he still adored her. She picked up the platter of sausages and began to pass them.

I mixed up the pancake batter and heated up the griddle. The sun poured in through the open windows as it sizzled.

As I stood, the soft, breeze of early morning drifting in, the scent of wild rose and lavender with it, I saw a purple blossom, deep and vibrant, sunbeams playing along its heart shaped leaves.

"The lilac bush is blooming," I said.

Everyone sat silent, Mama's thoughts so far away, a smile creeping softly across Mai Li's face.

Mai Li would never know Georgie or Anh Ly. But, a mother's love can reach across an ocean and a father's from the grave.

As we finished, Carrie and I cleaning up, Will and Jamie left to tinker with Jamie's truck, Carrie took the children out to play, and Mama took to her bed for a late morning nap.

I stood alone with my thoughts.

I was certain Will would discover something important. Despite his makeshift lab out in the middle of nowhere, according to his colleagues, he had an observant eye.

I must remember to take Will a midday meal. He would be forgetting the time.

I would wash his test tubes, polish up the microscopes, and pore over the latest journals with him.

The house was full of ancestral spirits. We come into the world alone, as common wisdom has it, but we come bound by the deeds and courage, the hopes and dreams, the joys and sorrows of our ancestors.

I gathered up the picnic basket filled with Will's lunch, his favorite cheeses and sausages, and a thermos of hot chocolate.

I set out across the meadow, rain clouds forming above, my feet as bare as the day I was born. I could feel the baby stirring within me. I picked up my pace to reach the door of the lab before the storm clouds broke.

Jan Surasky has worked as a writer for a San Francisco daily newspaper. Her many articles and short stories have been published in national and regional magazines and newspapers. She has also taught writing at a literary center and a number of area colleges near her home in upstate New York. Her award-winning novels include *Rage Against the Dying Light*, *Back to Jerusalem*, and *The Lilac Bush is Blooming*.